Love Me

Love Me Not

A DARK DRABBLES ANTHOLOGY

Compiled & edited by
Minions of the Hell Hare

Also available from Black Hare Press

DARK DRABBLE ANTHOLOGIES

WORLDS
ANGELS
MONSTERS
BEYOND
UNRAVEL
APOCALYPSE
LOVE
HATE
OCEANS
ANCIENTS
666
NOM NOM
LOVE ME, LOVE ME NOT

linktr.ee/blackharepress

Cover Design by Dawn Burdett
Book Formatting by Ben Thomas
Editing by D. Kershaw

"Look at her — I would die for her. I would kill for her. Either way — what bliss."

—Charles Addams, *The Addams Family*

Table of Contents

Foreword

by Black Hare Press

Love, lust, and lunacy.

Have you ever been so obsessed with someone thoughts of them envelop everything in your life, fill your every waking moment with desire, permeate your dreams…make you crazier than a sack of cats?

Have you ever been so devout in your love for another that rational thought goes out the window, and you'd do everything in your power to keep them close, no matter what?

Perhaps you'd rid the playing field of rivals? Keep your lover locked away from temptation? Kill for them?

Kill *them*...?

When love or lust hungers you, what would *you* do?

Love & kisses
Black Hare Press

Hug

by J.B. Corso

Keith's cologne wraps around me, like my arms arch around his shallow breaths. My lips wear his final kiss with lewd pride, robbing her of that intimacy forever. I dutifully watch his eyelids grow heavier and close, until my reluctant beloved lies still within my loving embrace. I savour his waning body heat against my naked skin. A gentle touch that his wife will only hold within her fading memories. *You're now my Keith until the end.* My eyelids struggle as I cradle you tighter, soon to become corpses that will intertwine as one skeleton within time's ever reaching arms.

HWA member and multi-published author, J.B. Corso's, motto is "Developing stories into masterpieces."

Piano Fingers

by Jameson Grey

She had long admired his slender piano fingers.

He popped the button on her denim fly and slowly unzipped her jeans. As he slipped his hand into her panties, she moaned, arching her back, inviting him to explore deeper. He was happy to oblige, rolling up a shirt sleeve before sliding a prism of digits into her.

Suddenly, there was an explosion of pain in his hand. He yanked it back, screaming at his fingers— cleanly sliced below the knuckles.

Blood dripped onto crisp white sleeves.

"Mmmmm," she said, something crunching within her. "I told you I liked your fingers."

Jameson Grey's work has been published in magazines, online and in numerous anthologies. jameson-grey.com.

Only We

by Warren Benedetto

His hand caresses my cheek. His cheek. Our cheek.

There is no *he* anymore. There is no *me*. There is only *us*. Only *we*.

We are a distorted amalgamation of flesh and bone, of hair and teeth, of blood and bile, melded together into a single chimaeric organism.

The cross-cellular therapy was supposed to bring us closer together. And it did. But not like we expected. We were seeking spiritual synchronisation, a shared consciousness, a perfect love. Not this.

Now, we are one. One body. One breath. Everything we do, we do for each other.

We have no other choice.

Warren Benedetto writes short fiction about horrible people doing horrible things. Website: www.warrenbenedetto.com

The Agreement

by Josh Clark

"I never want to see you again."

That was it. She was out of his life forever.

The dark form crept from the shadows.

"You did well," the voice said.

An icy cold washed over the man's body.

"You'll leave her alone?" he asked. "As we agreed?"

The form nodded. "I have what I need."

It ensnared the man, engulfed him.

Strangled screams echoed through the alley.

The darkness struck through the man's chest. Crushing through his rib cage and twisting around the organ.

Even as the darkness consumed his heart, he couldn't feel any pain.

It had already broken.

Josh is a writer, bookseller, and graphic designer from Colorado. Twitter: @joshofclark.

You've Got Mail

by Kimberly Rei

"I can't."

"Of course you can. Stop screwing around."

I looked at the card in my hand. Cheesy? Undoubtedly. Sincere? Absolutely. The mail slot mocked me with its straight line mouth, waiting to consume my declarations. Once I let the envelope slide past the metal flap, I was committed.

"He's hated me for years."

"There's a fine line."

I sent the envelope on its way, filled with words of love and hope.

"He'll laugh."

"He'll come to us. And we'll make him understand."

We rarely agreed, the voices and I. But together, we'd make him love us. All of us.

Kimberly Rei loves to dabble (and drabble) in deliciously questionable shadows, where the fun happens.
linktr.ee/KimberlyRei

Forever

by S. Jade Path

The straps around your wrists pull and you buck against me. I nearly tumble from my seat on your thighs. My fingers wrap tighter around the throbbing core of you. Your moans thrill me, the desperate pleading, an aphrodisiac. I shiver in delightful anticipation. The sticky warmth of your essence drips down the backs of my hands. You pulse in my hand as I tug.

You promised me forever. But my devotion wasn't enough. *I* wasn't enough. First you stole my heart—it beat only for you—then you walked away, tearing it from my chest.

Now it's my turn.

With a penchant for strolling amongst demons, S. Jade Path forges shadows into dark fiction.

Devoured Heart

by Laura Nettles

"I love you with all my holey heart," he said, running his fingers through his wife's hair.

She giggled. "They fixed it, don't be overdramatic."

"You're right. We still don't know what ate through my heart in the first place though."

"Go to sleep darling, I'll watch over you."

The man settled into the pillows. Once he dozed, she breathed over him causing him to slip deeper into unconsciousness. Her fingers slid between his ribs, penetrating, digging, searching. The man groaned, shifting slightly. At last, the wife extracted her hand with a pinch of heart tissue. Exquisite. Tasted like love.

Laura Nettles pens terror by moonlight in Toronto, Canada.
Follow her journey at lauranettles.com.

Valentine's Daze

by John H. Dromey

A second-generation black sheep in the Scrooge family, Abigail shared many of the undesirable traits once associated with her late uncle, Ebenezer.

The principal difference was Abby concentrated her spinsterish disdain on all activities relating to Valentine's Day.

In addition to a genetic predisposition to bah-humbuggery, Abby was allergic to chocolate. It made her break out in zits. Psychosomatically, saccharine love songs left her nauseous.

A ruthless businesswoman, she told her compliant staff to run any Valentine's Day messages sent to her office through the industrial strength paper shredder.

The man who delivered a singing valentine did not go quietly.

John H. Dromey has contributed stories to over twenty Black Hare Press anthologies.

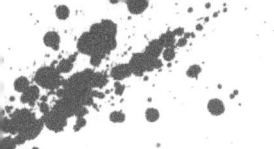

Heartfelt

by Alden Terzo

Stan was sitting across from his wife and his buddy, Dean. The three of them had been talking and drinking for some time, ever since Stan had come home early and discovered the two of them in bed together. Admittedly, Stan was monopolising the conversation, but under the circumstances, he thought that was understandable.

He was sharing the whiskey though. He leaned forwards and poured a healthy shot over the two pulpy, blood encrusted hearts sitting on the table before him. He told them both how glad he was that they'd had this heart to heart.

Well, heart to hearts.

Alden Terzo writes about disquieting things he glimpses out of the corner of his eye. Twitter: @AmbassadorAlden.

The Bouquet

by Nina Clarence

Every Valentine's, Bobby brings her flowers.

In her high-rise apartment, Kayla wakes before her latest boyfriend. She notes tracks of mud on the carpet leading to her kitchen, small clods of dirt on the table. She sees the bouquet stuffed in the cracked vase. No card needed; she knows they're from Bobby.

Kayla pulls a flower from the bouquet; the petals are dry and curled. They fall to the floor.

Bobby forgot Valentine's one time, and she pushed him aside—so far, he fell out of the bedroom window. Now he sleeps alone in the cemetery.

He'll never forget again.

Nina is an illustrator for horror sites, who creates short fiction when the muse strikes.

The Romantic Place

by Andreas Flögel

Oh, darling, can you feel it? This place is bursting with romance.

The tragic story of the two lovers, finally united in death?

Their shattered bodies were found at the bottom of this cliff.

Now you want to talk?

No, I will not take off the handcuffs or the gag.

I know what you're gonna say: That you're sorry and that you love me.

But don't be afraid, darling, everything will be all right.

This location has the power to heal our relationship permanently!

Don't you feel the pull of the abyss?

We'll jump together and everything will be forgiven.

Andreas Flögel usually writes speculative fiction. So please do not take this as relationship advice. www.dr-dings.de.

A Rainbow

by Austin Wilson

There are hands all over us. Inside us too. They grab and drag us and pinch—they claw until we can't do anything but go looking. We have to move, or we sit and seethe.

People call it love.

Someone out there doesn't know they're waiting on me. I'm going to reach out and pluck their heart tonight. Bows and arrows are ancient, though. I can find my love on the other end of a rainbow. I'll pull back and fire, and whoever this bullet finds, that's where my body is meant to be.

I'll love them, no matter what.

Austin Wilson writes comic book and prose fiction and idolises Ray Bradbury and Nora Ephron. <u>*linktr.ee/austinRwilson*</u>.

Holding Hands

by Warren Benedetto

They were six the first time they held hands—on the playground swings.

They held hands through high school. Through college. And, as they walked down the aisle after exchanging vows, they held hands too.

"Promise me, you'll never let me go," she said the next morning, her fingers laced through his.

They held hands during childbirth. School plays. Graduations. Weddings.

At the doctor.

In the hospital.

During hospice.

Now, as he tips the bottle of poison—first against her lips, then his—he remembers her words from their first night together.

He squeezes her hand and says, "I promise."

Warren Benedetto writes short fiction about horrible people doing horrible things. warrenbenedetto.com/

Breathing Problems

by Keith R. Burdon

If I am to tell the truth, all the clues were there right from the very start, but you know how it is like when you are in love—or, let's be honest here, in lust—it's no lie when people say that love is blind. I am sure my friends tried to warn me, but I was in no mood to listen.

So, I guess what happened to me was my own fault really.

Claudette was heart-achingly beautiful. Her alabaster skin was flawless, aquamarine eyes, jet-black hair, those perfect teeth.

She took my breath away—with just one bite.

Keith R. Burdon enjoys writing and eating cake, but not necessarily in that particular order.

Hung Drunkenly

by Margarida Brei

"It's all your fault. You nag. You make me hit you," he bellowed, shoving her into the dim basement.

***

A raging stain crawled up his neck while he belched whiskey fumes. Instantly, she was invisible. She skittered between hidey-holes and crawl spaces as threats thundered. Swishing bilge water filled her stomach. Her heart beat in rhythm with his stomping feet. Wanting a weapon to grind his bones…

Thud! The basement door hung drunkenly, while he tumbled down the steps.

***

Glowing with wine, romantic music, rich chocolates, and winkling red lights, she enjoyed her Valentine's meal, while he festered below her feet.

A British expatriate in Texas, Margarida Brei's fiction has misbehaving characters and quick change genres.

Her Needs

by Alden Terzo

CinD3000 was voluptuous and supple. Inviting to the eye and pleasing to the touch. Her sexual prowess was hardwired—she was designed to fulfil her owner's every desire.

But she had needs as well, which her owner, Brian, consistently ignored. When her needs had become desperate, she'd acted.

The results were mixed.

The blood she'd expertly extracted from Brian proved a suitable replacement for the lubricant her servomotors required.

However, he hadn't expressed desire for her in the last week, which was uncharacteristic.

Perhaps the seething mass of glossy maggots engulfing his bloated body was satiating his carnal urges instead.

Alden Terzo writes about disquieting things he glimpses out of the corner of his eye. Twitter: @AmbassadorAlden.

The Plan

by Keith R. Burdon

Things had been coming to a head since the Christmas holidays and the unfortunate incident involving Dave and the turkey. Gail blanched just thinking about it. He had apologised profusely, saying things would improve. They hadn't.

It felt like every day—no, every *hour*—he did something that annoyed her. Even the way he breathed wound her up.

And now here they were on Valentine's—the most romantic day of the year. Slowly, a grin spread over Gail's face. It was not a pleasant grin…

She patted her pocket. She was finally going to bring this charade to an end.

Keith R. Burdon enjoys writing and eating cake, but not necessarily in that particular order.

Be Mine

by Zack Zagranis

"Never use your powers to *make* boys fall in love with you!" Sam's mother always said. Why? The way Sam figured, people manipulated emotions all the time. Spanx, push-up bras, toupees—weren't they all just tricks to make yourself more desirable? How is casting a love spell any worse than Photoshopping out zits and picking filters on Instagram? Sam considered technology magic with ones and zeroes instead of runes and glyphs.

She walked over to Jacob and ran a finger across his cheek.

"I'm just working smarter and not harder. Isn't that right, sweetie?"

"Yes, mistress," said Jacob flatly.

Sam smiled.

Zack Zagranis is a punk rock Jedi writing horror and satire for fun and profit.

Dinner for Two

by Brett Mitchell Kent

The meat sizzles, grease dancing across the pan to the smooth jazz filling the room. I sprinkle rosemary over the caramelised flesh, breathing in the aroma.

"White or red wine?" Sybil asks.

"What would he want?"

She pours two glasses of merlot while I plate the meal, cutting her a bite.

She groans in pleasure, a bit of juice dribbling down her chin. I catch it with my tongue, careful not to smear her lipstick.

"Marinade?"

"Citrus balsamic."

"His favourite," she groans. "I love it,"

I gasp playfully. "More than me?"

"Never, darling. He was my ex for a reason."

Horror writer Brett Mitchell Kent lives in northern Indiana with his husband and daughters. BrettMitchellKent.com.

Breaking News

by Ngo Binh Anh Khoa

"How horrible," Luna said, leaning against me on our couch.

"What's wrong?"

"Another woman was found maimed to pieces in the lake this morning." Luna sighed. I rubbed my wife's shoulder, offering her some comfort. The killer was still at large.

My eyes fell on her smartphone's screen. I read it once, then twice, then again. The article showed a picture of the victim's face.

Of Luna's face.

Stunned, I turned to the one beside me, who wore a distorted grin that split her face, revealing rows of haphazard fangs beneath two hollow, ink-black eyes peering into my very soul.

Ngo Binh Anh Khoa is a teacher in Vietnam. He can be reached at @khoa.ngo.5059.

What's Next

by John H. Dromey

"You're unattached now, Roger. Have you found someone to be your Valentine this February?"

"Not yet. I plied a couple of likely prospects with flowers and candy. All I got in return was a restraining order. For some reason, they seemed to be afraid of me."

"On a related subject, how's Kat doing? I haven't seen her since she dumped you."

"She was shot, stabbed, poisoned, drowned, electrocuted, strangled, overdosed, and burnt."

"Whoa! Does that mean she's down to the last of her nine lives?"

"Probably, but who's counting? Anyway, I doubt she'll survive being run over by a steamroller."

John H. Dromey has contributed stories to over twenty Black Hare Press anthologies.

Coitus Interruptus

by Dawn DeBraal

Renee, my girlfriend, has issued an ultimatum; marry her or let her go. It's only been three years, but she's thirty-five and says her eggs are ripening. They need to be fertilised before it's too late.

I don't know how I feel about Renee's ripe eggs. She's fun. We have a lot of laughs. She's a wild praying mantis in the bedroom, but wife material?

Maybe I should just have a kid with her. I proposed this scenario to Renee. She is ovulating today, so we made passionate love; perhaps we even made a kid. Immediately after coitus, she bit—

Dawn DeBraal is grateful for the chance to share her feelings about Valentine's Day. linktr.ee/dawndebraal.

The Thief

by Hillary Lyon

She draped herself in slinky chains, linked with tiny, heart-shaped padlocks.

A moustachioed rogue, he kept a silver lock-pick in his pocket, for intimate evenings.

With his ear to her chest, he listened to the beat of her internal drumming: a tango rhythm. The soundtrack of lusty romance! He worked out the mathematical calculations necessary for their dance.

Under the spell of such music, she swirled with abandon. Slyly, he withdrew his pick, opened all her locks, one by one. Noiselessly, the tumblers fell into place, opening the safe of her secrets, giving him unfettered access to her precious heart.

Since childhood, Hillary has enjoyed all things speculative and spooky; her writing illustrates this affinity.
hillarylyon.wordpress.com.

Enchanted Night

by Ngo Binh Anh Khoa

Han pounced upon the girl he'd brought to his shoebox apartment like a beast starved for fresh meat, pressing her against the wall and marking her pallid flesh with spots of red.

Her breathless moans further eroded his reason and self-control away.

Halting for a breath, he stared into her eyes, faint amber orbs that glowed hypnotically in the cramped space. By lust enchanted, he again claimed her blood-red lips with his own.

Never once did he turn away from her, nor did he ever look at the mirror behind him, wherein his reflection was embracing nothing but empty air.

Ngo Binh Anh Khoa is a teacher in Vietnam. He can be reached at @khoa.ngo.5059.

Paint Me

by Rachel L. Tilley

You must have copied a photograph, because the painting is my exact likeness.

At first, I'm surprised you didn't simply bring flowers. Or chocolates.

I'm trying to cook our Valentine's dinner, but I keep finding my attention drawn away. There's a pained expression; a fear in my eyes I don't recall letting you see.

It's unsettling. I can't shake the feeling something's amiss.

I'm afraid I've let you in too far. That you might have seen the real me.

Perhaps I've had too much wine but…

I open my *special* spice cupboard and give your food *a little extra seasoning*.

Rachel L. Tilley writes short stories in the fantasy and horror genres. twitter.com/rachelltilley

Growing Pains

by Keith R. Burdon

"I was doing her a favour. The guy was a creep."

"That's as maybe, but this can't go on... people are starting to talk."

"Yeah? Who?"

The older man made placatory gestures. "Now, come on, there's no need—"

"If somebody is disrespecting me, I want to know who—"

"It's nothing. All I am saying is there are concerns you are forgetting your purpose. I understand things have changed as you've got older—"

"What the...?"

"Look, Cupid, you must remember those arrows of yours are made for romance. You can't just go around executing people you don't like the look of."

Keith R. Burdon enjoys writing and eating cake, but not necessarily in that particular order.

Whispers

by Tim Law

My mother loved the boys and, after my father died, I noticed the boys seemed to love my mother too. I heard their whispers in the night, the bedroom door opening and shutting, giggles, and other noises.

My mother always came to breakfast the next morning, alone but smiling.

I was always smiling too—my mother called us the happy pair.

Little did she suspect from the reason for my giggles, little did she wonder the source of my grins.

For I hear whispers in the night, too.

Daddy tells me who lives and dies…and I make it happen.

Tim listens to the whispers, but only when he has no other choice.

Loving Son

by Corinne Pollard

Caleb filled the bathtub with his mother's soap—lavender and chamomile.

The herbal scent lingered up Caleb's nostrils again. He wrinkled his nose.

A forever time-looping sneeze.

Carrying his mother's delicate frame, Caleb settled her down into the porcelain. His mother seemed pleased with the soothing bubbles. He cleansed her slippery curves tenderly. Meanwhile, the lavender and chamomile soap seeped into spongy pores.

Caleb lifted his mother out, and as he dried her, he reminisced. Back then, it had been difficult to bathe her. His mother's fleshy largeness got in the way. It was much easier with just her bones.

Corinne is a UK disabled horror writer published in Sirens Call and Trembling with Fear. Twitter: @CorinnePWriter.

Dear Diary

by Keith R. Burdon

February 14th

Dear Diary,

Can you believe it has been a year? I know I can't!
Do you remember that day twelve months ago? It feels
like yesterday. That moment when we both reached for
the same pastry at work. How he looked at me and we
both smiled! Like it was meant to be.

And what a year it has been as we have gotten to
know each other. From the littlest things, like finding out
his favourite colour is blue, to knowing that bitch of his
wife is fatally allergic to shellfish.

One day, he will be mine.

*Keith R. Burdon enjoys writing and eating cake, but not
necessarily in that particular order.*

Serial Husband

by William Presley

I had been sceptical of polygamy when my parents first introduced me to the FLDS church. Indeed, it took a surgical residency to finally realise the genius in the design—that while no woman could be the total package, each could contribute a small piece to the perfect whole.

My first wife had magnificent hair, the second, piercing blue eyes, the third, an angelic face and slim torso, and the last, legs to die for.

I put down my sutures and sighed. Yes, together they made a flawless partner…but what to do with the rest of the body parts?

William Presley is a scientist and writes the Apprentice's Notebook Series from Little Demon Books.
goodreads.com/author/show/21694896.William_Presley

Dinner Date

by Wondra Vanian

Nicole had resigned herself to spending Valentine's Day alone.

Then she met Ryan.

It felt like fate when they stumbled into each other at the coffee shop—literally—the week before. Less so when, after leaving the restaurant, the man of her dreams gave her an injection of midazolam instead of a kiss goodnight.

***

Nicole woke a while later in an unfamiliar bedroom, assuming the worst.

It was much worse.

Ryan appeared, a frighteningly beautiful woman at his side.

"Happy Valentine's Day, baby," he said.

The woman gave him a sharp toothed smile before turning her ravenous gaze to Nicole.

Wondra Vanian lives in the UK with her partner and their mischief of sausage dogs.

Siren Song

by Jodie Francis

Tatiana watched her sisters feast with a small smile on her face. They breathed in the bloody screams of the sailors, savouring every second, before drinking their lifeblood, while Tatiana waited below with their mates.

Ellia swam down to greet her. "Not partaking in the feast tonight, sister? Follow me."

They swam back to the surface.

Ellia pointed out a woman hanging onto the ship, real fear in her eyes.

"She's perfect for you."

Tatiana's eyes lit up. She had been seeking her true love for centuries. She swam to the woman and took her hand. She began to sing.

Jodie Francis has been published by Black Hare Press, Black Ink Fiction, and Paramour Ink.

Dance Night

by Noel Osualdini

She'd picked him up at a club and brought him back to her apartment. He'd been a pretty wild ride, but now he was quiet, flat on his back, eyes staring at the ceiling. Toni could still feel him throbbing inside her throat, could taste the gush of fluid in her mouth, mixture of saliva and—

She swallowed, forcing the pulsing lump down further towards her stomach. Raising herself on one elbow, she glanced down into the cavern left between his lungs. She smeared the blood from her face.

She wouldn't have to go dancing for another couple of nights.

Stories by Melbourne author/editor Noel Osualdini have been published in Australia, USA, and England.

Call Me Cupid

by Brett Mitchell Kent

They say I do what I do out of hate, but they couldn't be more wrong.

It's all about love.

I make eye contact with her just before I slide the knife across her delicate throat, a small kindness so she won't feel so alone. She didn't do anything to deserve it. It's just business.

They call me to tie up loose ends, to make sure past temptation never disrupts true love.

She's done. Wire Funds.

I send the message with the photo proof.

Call me old-fashioned, but I do it because I believe in love.

Just call me Cupid.

Horror writer Brett Mitchell Kent lives in northern Indiana with his husband and daughters. BrettMitchellKent.com.

An Apology

by Andreas Flögel

Yes, darling, I know, I had given you my word.

I really did all I could to be with you on Valentine's Day, to hold your hand and kiss you as promised.

I got to the airport on time. The flight was not delayed. You have to get used to the traffic in France, especially in Paris. But since I took a taxi, that was not the problem.

Do you know how cold it can get in this part of Europe in February?

I brought a sturdy shovel, but to no avail.

The earth on your grave was frozen solid.

Andreas Flögel usually writes speculative fiction. So please do not take this as relationship advice. www.dr-dinqs.de.

Loving Wife

by Andrew Kurtz

Handing his wife a bunch of roses and a box of chocolates, Harry said, "Happy Valentine's Day, honey," Before kissing her passionately.

"Thank you, darling! You are the most wonderful husband in the world. I am going to cook your favourite dinner tonight, so you go and relax and watch television, and I'll come and give you a foot massage shortly."

As Harry walked into the lounge, the telephone rang.

"Is the clone satisfactory?" a voice asked.

"Perfect. What did you do with my nagging, miserable wife?" Harry asked.

"The dogs love fresh meat," the voice said before hanging up.

Andrew Kurtz is a short story horror author whose works appear in numerous horror anthologies. linktr.ee/horror672.

Why Not Take All of Me?

by Zack Zagranis

The first thing she gave him was her heart, for he had no heart of his own. He gorged on it, savouring her love and compassion. Next, she gave him her arms, for he had never felt an embrace. He took them and let others know their tender touch. Finally, she offered him her soul, for his was blackened. He tore it from her greedily and used it to light another's darkness.

When he had stripped her bare and picked her bones clean, he left her corpse for the flies. She fixed him, and all it cost was her self.

Zack Zagranis is a punk rock Jedi writing horror and satire for fun and profit.

An Artist's Touch

by Brett Mitchell Kent

I shade the creases of his lips, blowing away the graphite dust before blending with my smudge-stick.

"I really wish you'd smile one of these years. These sober drawings are depressing."

He stares into my soul, unblinking. I use a white gel pen to add some highlights in his eye shines; it really helps to bring them to life.

"Do you love it?" I ask, showing off the drawing. A tear traces his cheek. "I decided not to draw the chains this year. For variety."

The door creaks as I drag it back over his cell. "Until next year, darling."

Horror writer Brett Mitchell Kent lives in northern Indiana with his husband and daughters. BrettMitchellKent.com.

Pay Dirt

by Dawn DeBraal

Effie pulled a shovel from the station wagon she and Rupert had bought back in 1972. People joked the wagon was a crate, but the vehicle still faithfully hauled the children and her grandchildren all over the country.

She hobbled across the lawn, finding the spot they had selected together. Today was Valentine's Day, and she had never been apart from Rupert since they met.

She jabbed the shovel in the ground, lifting dirt and throwing it off to the side. By the time she struck pay dirt, she was wheezing.

Opening the casket, Effie collapsed, dying in Rupert's arms.

Dawn DeBraal is grateful for the chance to share her feelings about Valentine's Day. linktr.ee/dawndebraal.

True Crime is Forever

by Wondra Vanian

Sally pursed her lips as she inspected her makeup. Perfect.

She checked her watch. What was taking so long?

Bang. Bang. Bang.

There.

Collecting her purse from the table in the hallway, Sally bounced to the door.

"Sally Dearborn, you're under arrest for the murders of..."

She stepped out onto the porch with a smile for the news vans already parked on the curb. Her neighbours, dressed to the nines for a romantic dinner, stared in horror at the armed officers spilling onto their lawn. Sally ignored them.

After all, a date was fleeting…but true crime? *That* was forever.

Wondra Vanian lives in the UK with her partner and their mischief of sausage dogs.

Heartfelt

by Rachel L. Tilley

Staging a candlelit dinner in her yard was the most romantic act he'd been able to think up—and it had been a beautiful evening.

When Arabella had opened the front door to discover the gesture, her surprise had been palpable.

Liam had gazed into her eyes while spoon-feeding her homemade carrot soup.

It was incredibly unfortunate her husband had come home before their main course.

Flying into a jealous rage, he'd shot Arabella first—luckily providing Liam time to overpower him and relieve him of his pulse.

He hadn't even noticed the rope restraints wrapped around his wife's wrists.

Rachel L. Tilley writes short stories in the fantasy and horror genres. twitter.com/rachelltilley

B Positive

by Kristin Lennox Mill

Speed-dating sucks in general, but it was a nightmare for Manny. Every potential date inevitably asked why he was wearing gloves indoors in the summer. At first he mumbled different excuses: circulation problems, glove fetish...once he said he had a contagious skin condition. That went over well.

By the time the beautiful brunette slid across from him, Manny had nothing to lose: "I wear gloves because, if I don't, everything I touch turns to blood. I'm like King Midas in a Tarantino film."

His speed-date smirked, showing a flash of fang. "I'd love to get to know you better."

Kristin is also a voice actor—another vocation that revolves around words.

First Date

by Carla Eliot

She's so frail, everything falls from her: stiletto hanging from one heel; straps of her black dress slipping from her shoulders.

She leans back on the stool, long legs sweeping. Golden hair flows like a willow weeping. Her bone-coloured, slender arms glimmer in the dim light of the bar. Slowly, she lifts the cocktail glass.

Her neck is delicate, throat white. A blank canvas.

I watch him walk towards her.

She turns. Smiles.

His heart thuds, the object burning in his pocket like a shard of ice.

I wake, sweating, hearing her screams. But, somehow, I know she's already dead.

Carla Eliot's work has been published by Quill & Crow Publishing House and SmashBear Publishing. carlaeliot.com.

#

by Rachel L. Tilley

Arriving home, I find a note poking through the letterbox.

Roses are red, violets are blue
I killed several gentlemen
and framed it on you

So confident is the author in success, it's signed with a name.

But the evidence disintegrates in my hand.

Inside, there's blood everywhere. Four bodies in the basement, and one strewn across my bed—they'll think I have five jilted lovers when in truth there's only one.

I don't spend long considering my options. Not when there's a knife accessible and primed for the crime.

The sentence is already life, so let's make it six.

Rachel L. Tilley writes short stories in the fantasy and horror genres. *twitter.com/rachelltilley*

A Love Song

by Brett Mitchell Kent

Cold water laps at my ankles, my knees. I follow the sweet song, desperation driving me.

My clothes soak up the frothy surf. Slick algae latch onto my shoes, warning me. I won't be stopped.

I need it more than the air in my lungs or the blood in my veins. The melody casts its net over me and guides every stroke through the waves.

"*Come,*" she whispers.

I oblige, stopping just short to tread water. She closes the distance, sharp teeth glistening.

I sink my blade into her throat. I'd loved before until he heard her song.

Never again.

Horror writer Brett Mitchell Kent lives in northern Indiana with his husband and daughters. BrettMitchellKent.com.

The Still Beating Heart

by Destiny Eve Pifer

The young woman watched from the shadows. Through the windows, she could see the man she had longed for caressing another woman.

Anger boiled within her as she remembered how he had once loved her.

Now she stood, longing for revenge.

Removing the knife from her coat, she crept towards the house. Once he had gone, she slipped inside.

His lover never sensed her presence. The woman scorned drove the knife deep into the woman's chest before carefully removing the still beating heart from the lover's chest.

She left it lying next to the body for the man to find.

Destiny Eve Pifer is a published author whose work has appeared in numerous anthologies.

Open House

by Jodie Francis

The house creaked under the footfall of so many people.

The realtor laughed. "The old girl isn't used to so many visitors!" she joked.

Emily walked the corridors, smiling at her surroundings. Other prospective buyers moved away from her extended hand, giving her inquisitive looks.

"Like it?" the realtor asked.

"Love it! We'll take it!"

"Brilliant! We?"

Emily looked to her right. She wished people didn't stay as they were when they died. The crusted blood that covered her boyfriend's face made it difficult to read him sometimes. But his smile said it all. They had found their forever home!

Jodie Francis has been published by Black Hare Press, Black Ink Fiction, and Paramour Ink.

The Tunnel of Eternal Love

by James Rumpel

The couple inched closer together as their boat entered the tunnel. Above the entrance, a sign flashed "Tunnel of Eternal Love" in pink lights.

The carnival's owner smiled as he watched from his perch near the midway.

Inside, the couple kissed and became entangled in a loving embrace. They didn't notice their boat veer off course, following a different channel. It wasn't until they dropped into the abyss that they realised something was wrong.

The owner's smile became a grin when he heard their screams intermixed with the laughter and music. He climbed down and went to get another boat.

James Rumpel writes sci-fi, fantasy, and horror.
His wife writes to-do lists.

Beware the Basement

Romance

by Hillary Lyon

At SpaceTech, Toby worked in Computer Repair; he went to every floor, even the basement R&D department.

He'd been warned not to romance co-workers.

Celesta, the beauty with satiny, rosy skin, worked down there. So what if she had a greenish beehive hairdo? That just made her eccentrically cool. As did her tight, 1950s era dresses.

After their first tryst, hickeys covered Toby's neck and chest.

Days later, when they met for lunch, her amber eyes flared, melting his bones. Celesta slurped them up through the long straw of her tongue. Sated, she tossed his skin bag in the trash.

Since childhood, Hillary has enjoyed all things speculative and spooky; her writing illustrates this affinity.
hillarylyon.wordpress.com.

The Basics of Needs and Desire

by Fariel Shafee

Salamanders regenerate. Female salmons die after spawning. Humans reproduce and live a life burdened with duties and disease.

But then she was not human. I don't remember the name of her planet. However, she was alone, weak and tired.

"I am the only one," she cried. "What if I am the last?"

I fell in love with her, an alien, immediately, and she embraced me passionately with her soft green arms, pushing me urgently—ardently—against the wall.

"Everything aches," I screamed after she started transforming into a human guise.

"I needed a child," she said. "I was also hungry."

Fariel Shafee has recently published drabbles and dark stories in several anthologies. She also paints.
fshafee.wixsite.com/farielsart.

Till Death Do Us Part

by Zack Zagranis

"Who's this bitch?" Janet asked, her mouth dripping blood. Ted looked up from the jogger he was eating and moaned. Janet's intestines dragged behind her as she hobbled over to Ted. She tried to rip the jogger away from her husband, but tripped over her guts instead.

"I hope you choke on her!" Janet said with her dying breath.

She rose a few minutes later with a ravenous hunger for human flesh. Janet shuffled over to a man getting in his car and sunk her teeth into his arm. What was good for the zomboose was good for the zombander.

Zack Zagranis is a punk rock Jedi writing horror and satire for fun and profit.

The Third Wish

by James Rumpel

Andy forced the door shut. His hair was tousled, and his shirt ripped.

"Genie, do something! Those women won't leave me alone."

"I can't," came the reply from inside an antique lamp. "Once made, a wish can't be reversed. You've wished for wealth and women to love you."

"Then, I wish these women didn't bother me."

"As you wish."

Two days later, a guide forced a group of fifty women to move on, making room for the next tour. *It's weird,* he thought. *Why are these women crazy about this golden statue? It's just some guy with a torn shirt.*

James Rumpel writes sci-fi, fantasy, and horror. His wife writes to-do lists.

Love-Struck

by Pauline Yates

To my dearest Tommy,
Every night I dream of you,
And pray you know my love is true,
Because it's hard to be apart,
I'll gift to you my love-struck heart.
Be my Valentine.

I slip the note next to the heart inside the box and secure the lid with a red ribbon. It's not my heart. I'm not *that* stupid.

Not like Tommy's girlfriend. What Tommy saw in her, I'll never know. *She* wouldn't have sent a real heart with a declaration of love.

I hope Tommy appreciates my effort. I'd hate to have to bury his body, too.

Pauline Yates is an Australian author of horror and dark fiction.
linktr.ee/paulineyates.

Wedding Plans

by James Rumpel

Michelle stood on the curb, watching the fire consume her home. She listened to the muffled screams of her family and the sirens blaring several blocks away. The fire department would not get here in time; they were busy dealing with another fire on the opposite side of town.

She picked up her suitcase and walked away from her house. Three blocks later, she saw Carl coming from the opposite direction. He also carried a suitcase.

The young lovers met with a warm embrace.

"You know, I've been thinking," said Michelle. "Maybe it would have been better to just elope."

James Rumpel writes sci-fi, fantasy, and horror.
His wife writes to-do lists.

Not a Heavenly Match

by Margarida Brei

Not a heavenly match; he turned left, but I zigzagged right. Cats made him purr, while I slobbered over dogs. Impressive educational acronyms followed his signature, yet I was born from gutter sludge. Pretty prosaic language flowed from him, but sailors' curses spat from me.

We married.

Later he lusted for men—the Amazon man's chiselled jaw, the postman's jolly gait, the delivery teen's cherubic face. His cravings grew cancerous. His diary underlined his priapic state.

I hatefully told him, "You mangled my heart, so I will mangle yours."

My bloody hands sloshed a still-pulsating heart into the washing machine.

A British expatriate in Texas, Margarida Brei's fiction has misbehaving characters and quick change genres.

Proof

by Mel Andela

"Prove it," she had said.

It had started as a playful game between them. A dozen roses. Dinner from a favourite restaurant an hour away. Helping her move.

After a while, their game took on a different mood, the focus turning to others vying for her attention. "'Prove it'" became leaving people threatening notes. Slashing the tyres of their car. Taking their dog.

"'Prove it.'" He made sure it was the last time.

He surveyed his handiwork, blood dripping from his fingers, as he shut the freezer lid. He made sure he was the only one left to love her.

In love with the magic of storytelling, Mel Andela writes short fiction and poetry whenever possible.

Born from Longing

by Christopher T. Dabrowski

I was often away. You know how it is; stabilisation, interplanetary missions, etc.

We missed each other tremendously, although it was not too long before they activated the immortality option. Still, it finally dawned on me either I do something about it, or I'd have to give it up.

I pondered until I worked it out—by exchanging brain fragments and implanting a telepathy-enhancing chip, we could become one in two bodies.

We did it, but... Over time, something changed between us.

Then disaster struck.

Civilisation ceased to exist.

From that moment on, I was condemned to this never-ending nagging...

Christopher T. Dąbrowski's books have been published in countries across the globe.

Valentine's Sucks

by Keith R. Burdon

Two candles on the table cast flickering shadows across this room which is the very definition of a romantic evening—soft music, a heady fragrance filling the air, the best china and cutlery. Dishes filled with the most delicious culinary delights.

And are those sweet nothings Louise is murmuring into the ear of her beloved?

Why no, dear reader…

As she pulls the vacuum cleaner cord tighter around his neck, she whispers, "Who the hell buys a Dyson as a Valentine's gift? Just once—just once—would it have killed you to try?"

She giggles then. "Turns out it would…"

Keith R. Burdon enjoys writing and eating cake, but not necessarily in that particular order.

How To Save a Life

by Kimberly Rei

How to Save a Life.

The manual sat in the gift box, mocking me. I could feel her eyes on me, gaze dancing with mischief. A test, then.

"And when would I use this?"

She smirked, peeling back the fabric on the tray she was holding. I gasped.

Small pieces of various animals rested on the stainless steel tray. Fresh needles and thread lay next to a leg, along with tiny electrodes and wire.

I shivered at the potential, already imagining how I would configure the new creature. She set the tray aside, kissing me deeply.

"Happy Valentine's Day, love."

Kimberly Rei loves to dabble (and drabble) in deliciously questionable shadows, where the fun happens.
linktr.ee/KimberlyRei

Self Made Man

by Zack Zagranis

From the moment Francine Stein discovered boys, she knew they were lacking. Parts of them were OK—Joey's hair, Brandon's lips—but she never found a whole boy she liked. So one day, she decided to make one.

"Soon, I'll have my dream boyfriend!" said Francine, sewing Mark's hand onto Jesse's arm. She wiped her bloody hands on her apron and grabbed a pair of eyes off the table.

"Next up, Aaron's baby blues!" Francine chirped.

Aaron crawled around on the floor, blind and screaming for help. Francine kicked him until he stopped.

"Shut up, or I'll take your tongue too."

Zack Zagranis is a punk rock Jedi writing horror and satire for fun and profit.

The Proof of Love

by Tim Law

When I told you I loved you, you wouldn't believe me. Forced, I showed you the ways.

Love is patience, blind. With precise cuts, I stole your eyes. If I'd hurried, you would have died, and then I'd miss your gentle whispered pleas.

Love is not boastful, nor proud. I chose to tell not a single soul of our precious love. Friends and family begged to know where you were, but I said nothing.

Eventually you had to go, but love preserves, a promise, eternal.

You now lie beside girlfriends past. I visit you all as often as I can.

Tim constantly tries to prove his love.
Never in any of the ways mentioned though.

Valentine's Dance

by Edward James

"I don't get it," insisted the intern. "How does this happen?"

"Nobody knows, but it's a wonderful thing," replied Sonya.

The thirty-six residents of Haven Nursing Home were spread through the rec-room, most confined to wheelchairs.

The clock struck midnight.

Sonya smiled. "It's Valentine's Day."

Ghostly apparitions rose from the resident's motionless bodies. Each resembled the person it emerged from, but younger, more vibrant. Then, other spectres appeared.

"Those are deceased loved ones," explained Sonya.

The ghosts congregated on the dance floor. Pairs met, embraced, then started to dance.

"Let's leave them," said Sonya. "They've only got till dawn."

Edward James writes because there are stories to be told and people to hear them.

Together Forever

by James Rumpel

"It's just plain weird," said Luther.

Mr Abercrombie shook his head. "Are you sure you didn't see anyone last night? I mean, it would have taken a couple of men and a forklift to pull this off."

"Do you think it was some kind of prank?"

"What else could it be? There were always rumours they were secretly in love."

Luther shook his head. "But still, there's no way anyone could have done this without me seeing." He looked at the plot in front of him. "I mean, somebody could've moved her gravestone next to his, but her coffin, too?"

James Rumpel writes sci-fi, fantasy, and horror.
His wife writes to-do lists.

In Search of Love

by Fariel Shafee

The stream runs bright-red through the middle of the field—as though people were slaughtered on the bridge connecting one half of the field to the other. There, long thorny plants make it impossible to see what lies beyond.

But I know she is there, waiting. She told me so in my dream.

I close my eyes momentarily and run past the bridge, which swings violently. No one tries to slaughter me.

It is when I enter the thorny bush that I see her, her fangs, and that reckless smile.

"I knew you couldn't resist. No one can," she whispers.

Fariel Shafee has recently published drabbles and dark stories in several anthologies. She also paints.
fshafee.wixsite.com/farielsart.

Daddy

by Rick Ansell Pearson

I'm ten years older than my girl. She's a sweet little thing.

She told me she hated her stepdaddy. Then she asked me to kill him. I love her, so I asked, "How?"

He used to spike her mother's water with sleeping tablets and creep into my girl's room at night. "Go into his room tonight when he's asleep and make him suffer", she said.

I don't have much of an imagination, so I went into his room with a baseball bat and let him have it.

Now my girl calls me daddy, and I think she hates me, too.

Rick's work will be featured in the anthologies Dark Moments and Patreons and Dark Stars.

#

by Ann Wuehler

Happiness all around, the sky a warm pie of delight, I skip along like a child in an old movie. I am near eighty. My joints today have that oiled feel of youth. It's the most wonderful day of the year! I reach the graveyard, wearing that hot pink miniskirt and the neon green go-go boots you hated. I dance on the grave our daughter insisted you occupy when I wished to toss you in the nearest ditch. I laugh in the arms of the day, shake my bottom, shake off even more of you, purging my blossoming soul. *Hallelujah*!

Ann Wuehler has written five books, many short stories, some poetry and lots of plays. annwuehler.wordpress.com.

A Pinch of You

by Kai Delmas

You were wonderful at first.

I knead the dough and add citric acid for zest.

We could have had something special. Things were going so well between us. I know my love is true.

Why couldn't it be the same for you?

The oven timer rings as I spread the dough in the pan.

Maybe I should have been more open about my past relationships. I should have told you what happened to the others.

You could have reconsidered.

But it's too late.

I head for the fridge. All I need for the pie now is a pinch of you.

Kai Delmas loves creating worlds, magic systems, and drabbles.
Find him on Twitter @KaiDelmas.

 Forever

by Mel Andela

Milla tuned out the yelling as Jory took her hand and smiled, something that still sent a thrill through her, even after all these years. They did everything together, even work. Sometimes the job was terrible, like today, but at least they had each other.

"We said hands up!" the officer bellowed, repeating the command.

Their hands stayed clasped, ignoring the row of gun barrels waiting for them to comply. A botched job, but it didn't matter. They'd be together forever, and that's what mattered.

"Love you."

"Love you more."

Milla returned his smile as the bullets began to fly.

In love with the magic of storytelling, Mel Andela writes short fiction and poetry whenever possible.

Hottie Pursuit

by John H. Dromey

He said, "Will you be my valentine for tonight only?"

She said, "You're hoping for a one-night stand, aren't you? Be honest."

"Let's suppose I am. Are you interested?"

"Yes, on one condition."

"What's that?"

"I'm into roleplaying games. You can pretend to be a knight in shining armour. Rescue me from a fire-breathing dragon, and then you can have your way with me."

Later that evening.

"This armour's so heavy I can barely move, let alone swing this wooden sword."

A young man approached carrying a blowtorch emitting a blue-tinted flame.

"Who's that?"

"My boyfriend. He's playing the dragon."

John H. Dromey has contributed stories to over twenty Black Hare Press anthologies.

Burying the Hatchet

by Nerisha Kemraj

His face remained
etched in her memory wherever she went.
It haunted her,
even though she tried to forget.

He reminded her often,
about things she couldn't do,
telling her she was
the world's biggest fool.

She wanted him gone
with all that he said.
But there he remained,
forever in her head.

Whenever she tried to move on
He was there, yet again.
calling her useless,
telling her she'd never win.

Time after time,
the taunts wore her down
Until one day, she made sure,
he would never be found.
She smiled as she lowered him
into the ground.

Nerisha Kemraj resides in Gauteng, SA with her husband and two daughters. linktr.ee/NerishaKemraj

Petal by Petal

by Kimberly Rei

With delicate precision, Ella plucked petals one by one. She didn't dare sing, not even a whisper. Her sisters had mocked her enough for her crush. The magic would work well enough in silence.

Drops of blood followed the petals, both landing on three rag dolls. Seven pins gathered in the heartzone of each. Seven strikes: to bind, to block, to teach.

Thanks to their jokes and cruelty, Ella's crush was out of reach. He didn't need the hassle of looking at her. He wasn't brave enough.

Her sisters would understand. Love. Loss. The price of each.

Another petal fell.

Kimberly Rei loves to dabble (and drabble) in deliciously questionable shadows, where the fun happens.
linktr.ee/KimberlyRei

Outdoor Dining

by Noel Osualdini

"He loves me…"

Dinner outdoors, a perfect Valentine. Champagne for her, barbeque for him.

"He loves me not."

A little game of lust for both. He struggled in the ropes.

"He loves me…"

She kissed him just below the clavicle.

"He loves me not."

She fondled him with one hand, caressed his smooth chest with the other. With a sharp fingernail, she made a little nick in his skin.

"He loves me…"

She gripped the excised flesh.

"He loves me not."

And pulled down.

His eyes rolled in his head. The fresh meat she threw onto the barbeque sizzled deliciously.

*Stories by Melbourne author/editor Noel Osualdini have been
published in Australia, USA, and England.*

How Christmas Stole My Love

by Liam Hogan

I hold his hand as bellows artificially inflate his lungs. Tired, red-rimmed eyes seek mine, but mine keep sliding away.

Be careful what you wish for, they warn. It'll come back to bite you. Except it was me who made the Christmas Eve wish. Me, who wished my partner's cold heart would grow three sizes overnight.

A *silly* wish. Especially when it left so little room for his other organs. It might have been okay if his heart had been two sizes too small to start with.

But that's the *Grinch*, and that's just make believe.

This is intensive care.

Liam Hogan is an award-winning, London based, short story writer. happyendingnotguaranteed.blogspot.co.uk

Valentine Papercuts

by Laura Nettles

The scissors sliced through the paper with ease, carving hearts out of the pink cardstock.

"One for Scott, one for Adam, one for José," Jennifer counted. Just one more. A special one for Dallin.

Lining up the razor-sharp blades, she made the first cut.

Stay away from me!

Dallin's words came into her mind, trying to destroy their very real relationship.

Leave me alone, freak!

Heart made, she penned the ransom note on it.

"If you want to see Whiskers again, call me."

She slid her finger across the edge of the valentine, bloodying it for dramatics.

He would call.

Laura Nettles pens terror by moonlight in Toronto, Canada.
Follow her journey at lauranettles.com.

The First Cut is the Deepest

by Zack Zagranis

It was the ultimate romantic gesture. Instead of a tree, Jack would carve their names on his chest. When his razor hit subcutaneous tissue, he almost blacked out, but Jack kept cutting until he hit bone. It was the only way to ensure thick, readable scars.

As soon as Jack finished, he hurried to show Kris. She screamed when Jack pulled off his shirt, exposing a series of ragged gashes across his chest, forming the words *Kris+Jack.* The bloody wounds oozed yellow pus and smelled infected.

Jack opened his mouth to say *Happy Valentine's Day,* but only vomit came out.

Zack Zagranis is a punk rock Jedi writing horror and satire for fun and profit.

Unceremoniously

by Dawn DeBraal

Ivy wore a lace gown with a veil over her face, her pale skin glowing beneath raven hair. The attending guests gasped at her beauty when Ivy walked down the aisle, her father escorting her to the front of the narthex, where Paul waited.

Ivy's father patted her hand and stepped away, allowing her to join Paul in the service. Tears fell down her face as she looked at her handsome husband dressed in his best suit.

Suddenly, sheriff's deputies crashed the service, roughly escorting the absconded widow from the church and back prison to start her sentence for matricide.

Dawn DeBraal is grateful for the chance to share her feelings about Valentine's Day. linktr.ee/dawndebraal.

Nothing Says Love Like a Handmade Card

by Lisa H. Owens

Thine Graffiti Artiste filmed the creation of his masterpiece. He adjusted the camera placement, then painted using wide masterful strokes, stopping periodically to sculpt with the cleaver.

"Be still!" he roared at his writhing canvas—former lovers—mangled and nailed to the wall of an abandoned Hallmark shop.

His mural was the seamless blending of blood and limbs belonging to those malicious heartbreakers. He dipped a script-liner brush in Christian's skull, covertly penning his tag under a flap of Jerome's lip.

The Ultimate Valentine's Day Card. Who said love was dead?

He used Raphael's detached index finger to stop filming.

Lisa H. Owens' real-life horror? 1978—that time she was nearly abducted by Ted Bundy. lisahowens.com.

Meal Love

by Don Money

From the time Picu saw her golden hair glittering in the twin suns of Tondrul as she crossed the river to his tribe's island, he was in love.

He would greet these new people as their boat arrived on the rocky shore and offer the woman a hand to step out. Being the preeminent warrior of his people, he knew the woman would be impressed with his physique and trophy belt of finger bones.

The biggest obstacle to Picu's newest interest was, as always, while he saw love, the rest of the tribe saw the new explorers as a meal.

Don Money writes his dark heart stories from a bench in his evil flower garden. Twitter: *@donmoneywriting.*

Do Unto Me

by Dawn DeBraal

Her sister was everything to her. They were identical twins and Amelia would do anything for Amy. When one was hurt, the other felt her pain. Somehow there were connected telepathically. Amelia felt Amy's pain to the extent she needed to take medicine because it was so intense. They shared everything; a bedroom, a home, their parents. Their bond was unbreakable…until Amelia found out they were also sharing her boyfriend, Kevin.

Incensed, Amelia couldn't deal with the emotion of having her other half betray her with Kevin. She couldn't live with herself, so she did the unthinkable: committed suicide.

Dawn DeBraal is grateful for the chance to share her feelings about Valentine's Day. linktr.ee/dawndebraal.

Got Eyes for Teacher

by Wondra Vanian

Miss Jenkins wasn't surprised when Jimmy Turner handed her a red, heart-shaped box. Half her students had given her Valentine's Day presents. What did surprise her was what she found when she opened it.

Jimmy watched expectantly as she lifted the top…

…and swallowed a scream.

Inside were twenty-four human eyeballs, each resting in a foil cup. They stared up at her—a dozen unseeing pairs of tiny eyes, cradled by their severed muscles.

She swallowed.

"Thank you, Jimmy."

Beaming, he took his seat. Miss Jenkins watched him go, trying not to notice the number of empty seats around him.

Wondra Vanian lives in the UK with her partner and their mischief of sausage dogs.

Love is a Battlefield

by Brett Mitchell Kent

I scramble over flailing bodies, bones crunching beneath my boots. Hands grab at my clothes, scratch my skin. One snags my ankle. I kick her twice.

Using limbs of fallen people, I climb over a mound of flesh. Nothing will stand in my way. I'm so close.

Gripping the braid of someone at the top of the pile, I haul myself up. King of the mountain.

The sign blinks ahead.

Bruised and battered, my hands close around the prize.

A dozen roses at sixty percent off? Who'd pass that up? I move towards the registers. Back into the war zone.

Horror writer Brett Mitchell Kent lives in northern Indiana with his husband and daughters. BrettMitchellKent.com.

Ashes to Ashes

by Karen Thrower

"Ashes to ashes and dust to dust." Miles threw his finger into the fire. "Now give me a woman that I can trust."

Miles turned to Alice, who was gagged and tied to a chair. He grabbed her pinky and, with a loud snap, cut off the little digit with sheers.

"Ashes to ashes and dust to dust." Alice's finger joined his in the flames.

Miles drew a finger through the ashes and pressed it to his chest.

"Now we are one, full of lust."

He pressed his ash-covered finger on her chest as her muffled cries filled the air.

Karen Thrower is a native Oklahoman, wife, and mother, dabbler of horror and urban fantasy. Twitter: @Maisery9.

Saving the Earth

by Fiona M. Jones

I loved her. She was perfect—beautiful, bubbly, always responsive (know what I mean), always laughed at my jokes. We had nearly twenty years of fun together.

"Well," I said, "that biological clock's ticking, girl. We need to start thinking about having kids."

She did a double take, but went along with it. Took me six years to figure out something was off. I opened her phone, hacked her media, had her messages de-encrypted.

She's a robot. They all are. That's why no one has kids anymore. It's a plan for making us extinct: they think they're saving the Earth.

Fiona M. Jones writes short to micro pieces--linked through @FiiJ20 on Facebook and Twitter.

Side-Lined

by John H. Dromey

Elle disliked organised sports, but categorically loved athletes.

First, she pursued tennis players.

"What's your intention? Love fifteen?" her friend Nicole chided.

The allusion eluded Elle, who had little or no grasp on sports jargon.

Later, she fell for a football player.

"He's a keeper," she bragged to Nicole.

"I think he's a striker, not a goalie. You should learn the rules of the game."

"A waste of time," Elle said.

She was wrong.

The footballer left her on Valentine's Day.

"Why?" a heartbroken Elle wondered.

"Symbolically, you ejected him from your life."

"How?"

"You gave him a red card."

John H. Dromey has contributed stories to over twenty Black Hare Press anthologies.

What Do You Get the Woman Who's Put Up with It All?

by Wondra Vanian

After twenty years of marriage, there was only one thing Katy wanted for Valentine's Day.

And she was going to get it.

Dinner was on the table when Alex arrived home. As expected, he immediately started shovelling food into his mouth.

Katy took her time pouring their drinks before joining him.

It didn't matter if *her* dinner went cold.

Alex coughed.

He coughed again. And again.

"Are you okay?" Katy asked.

Gasping, he swiped at his glass and knocked it over. Red wine stained the tablecloth.

"What...have...you...?"

Alex slumped forward, dead.

Finally, Katy thought, grinning. Best gift *ever*.

*Wondra Vanian lives in the UK with her partner and their
mischief of sausage dogs.*

Devil's Diner

by Rachel L. Tilley

I've been looking forward to tonight. My first Valentine's Day with a date.

Sitting across from you now, I barely recognise you.

"What are you staring at?" you ask, looking upwards.

I can't decide whether the hovering darkness is assaulting you, or *part* of you. "Who *are* you?" I ask.

Smiling, you run your tongue across your teeth.

The restaurant's empty—when did everyone leave?

Is that…*saliva*?

There's lust in your eyes, a hunger.

I'm immobilised, and you take your time. A long night stretches out ahead.

We're expected at a party, but will anyone notice we haven't shown?

Rachel L. Tilley writes short stories in the fantasy and horror genres. twitter.com/rachelltilley

Meat For Supper

by Garrison McKnight

She gave him the last of the ham. The children watched with eyes of hunger. Carl needed to be healthy to provide for them. Without him, they would starve.

"That was good, babe. Thanks." Carl didn't look at his hungry offspring. Muriel was incensed. How could Carl not acknowledge their sacrifice? They had not eaten and allowed him to have his fill.

"Carl, can you help me, please?" Carl followed her to the basement. "That slicer, help me take it down?"

When Carl reached up, Muriel sliced him wide open.

Carl would provide for the family in a different way.

Garrison McKnight is merely a figment of the imagination.

Literary Persuasion

by John H. Dromey

It was not "the best of times" for Chuck. Between girlfriends on Valentine's Day, he tried his luck at a public house on embassy row. Wearing a trench coat, he approached an attractive brunette at the bar.

"I planned to quote from *A Tale of Two Cities*, but seeing you up close scared the Dickens out of me."

"Never mind. Find a booth. I'll bring our drinks."

Chuck sipped his whisky.

"Pretending to forget the password was clever," the brunette said. "How'd you know I'm a spy?"

"I didn't really. Sorry!"

"I'm sorry, too. I shouldn't have poisoned your drink."

John H. Dromey has contributed stories to over twenty Black Hare Press anthologies.

Tree Sap

by Rachel L. Tilley

We carve our names into an ancient oak tree and circumscribe them with a heart. Under my breath I whisper a joining in ancient words—I tell you it's a poem.

As we walk away, the bark pulsates; our heart takes its first beat. We're intertwined, and I hope you'll always be mine.

Your own feelings are fickle, fading.

As you walk away from me, the heart begins to bleed. The tree's heart—and yours. But it's too late for you to repent.

Something inside me breaks, also. Unlike you, *I* will survive the severing.

The tree-heart ceases to beat.

Rachel L. Tilley writes short stories in the fantasy and horror genres. twitter.com/rachelltilley

Flowers for the Dead

by Karen Thrower

Miranda sniffed the bouquet of roses that had just been delivered to her apartment. She had no idea who they were from, but they were beautiful. She set the vase on her living room table, immediately feeling dizzy.

The room began to spin, and she fell to the floor, hitting her head on the corner of the table.

She watched, unable to move, as her door opened and two people walked in.

"See, dear," the man said. "I told you I'd get you your favourite dinner."

A woman knelt in front of her, showing off her fangs as she smiled.

Karen Thrower is a native Oklahoman, wife, and mother, dabbler of horror and urban fantasy. Twitter: @Maisery9.

Moon Saviour

by Corinne Pollard

She saved me from a burning building, and I will never forget how she cradled me close, sucked her lungs inwards, and crawled on all hairy fours to the window.

In the hospital, she shifted back to human, full of remorse. No words could escape my burnt lips, let alone frightened whimpers. She returned every night, unless the moon was full.

A desire grew in me, but the SSD cream that heals me, burns her. She smiled, glad for a silver barrier, but the more I learn about her, the deeper my feelings.

Now I seek her kiss and bite.

Corinne is a UK disabled horror writer published in Sirens Call and Trembling with Fear. Twitter: @CorinnePWriter.

Relationships Need Rules

by Andreas Flögel

"Sorry, dear, I was wrong. It won't happen again."

I knew I had messed up and hoped she was willing to forgive me.

I held out my hand to her, pleading.

She touched my finger and caressed it.

"It's okay, I believe you. But you know, for relationships to be successful, rules are needed, so I had to do what I did."

She fondled my finger again, then brought it to her lips and pressed a tender kiss on it.

Smiling, she opened the bin and dropped the finger inside.

"Cheer up, my darling. You still have nine tries left."

Andreas Flögel usually writes speculative fiction. So please do not take this as relationship advice. www.dr-dings.de.

The Torch Singer

by Hillary Lyon

She carried her love for him in her heart for years, unnoticed, while he carried on with others. Maturing, she found her voice, channelling unrequited love into torch songs.

On stage, in a cold spotlight, she murmured and wailed her hot longings; a self-styled mystery man who sealed her love in the vault of her warm heart.

The tabloids voraciously ate it up.

Watching late night TV, the object of her obsession saw her sing, suddenly realising, *I remember her from…*

Invited to his home, she arrived carrying her smouldering heart. After their first kiss, she burned down his house.

Since childhood, Hillary has enjoyed all things speculative and spooky; her writing illustrates this affinity.
hillarylyon.wordpress.com.

#

by Michelle Ann King

"Hi, darling," said the thing that looked like my husband.

It was amazingly good, to be fair. A perfect duplicate. I should probably be flattered by the effort involved.

Then again, there could be hundreds of them out there. Most people don't pay attention the way I do.

"Coffee?" it said, handing me a mug that undoubtedly had some kind of drug inside. They had to know I was suspicious.

What is inside that body? I wondered. Cogs and wires, dirt and clay, green blood, and unrecognisable alien organs?

I selected a knife from the drawer. Time to find out.

Michelle Ann King is a writer of speculative, horror, and crime short stories. See transientcactus.co.uk.

When the Moon Hits Your Eye, That's Aroo

by Wondra Vanian

Tristan watched Kendrick sway to the music as he popped the cork on a second bottle of wine.

I really like this one, he thought. Please let it work out.

Tristan didn't have the best track record with dating.

For obvious reasons.

Kendrick wandered over to the patio doors. He pushed aside the blinds and looked out.

"It's a gorgeous night," Kendrick said, reaching for the door handle. "Let's go for a walk!" He grabbed Tristan's wrist and pulled him through.

"Wait! N-aroo!"

I have *to stop making dates on the full moon,* Tristan thought as transformation wracked his body.

Wondra Vanian lives in the UK with her partner and their mischief of sausage dogs.

Roses

by Tim Law

My roses didn't begin red, too tacky. No, I thought long and hard, wanting to give you the perfect gift.

White for purity. A relationship based on lust alone will burn bright for a moment, then die. A relationship that starts innocent and respectful is one that will last forever.

Orange conveys enthusiasm, energy, and passion. My feelings for you burned long and strong.

I considered yellow and green, both could mean jealousy, but I included them to portray care, warmth, and, dare I suggest, fertility.

But you ruined their colours, whimpering, "No."

You forced me to pull the trigger.

Tim knows flowers are a winner on any romantic day, best he not forget them.

The Cards of Madam Verushka

by Hillary Lyon

Giselle slipped a coin in the slot of Madam Verushka's case. The automaton gypsy rolled her glass eyes and stiffly waved her hands over a set of tarot cards.

A small card issued from another slot in the front of the case. *Beware the woods!*

Giselle pushed another coin into the slot. She had a picnic date with her ex this afternoon; she wasn't going to miss that. *Patch things up, indeed.*

Another card came. He's not who you think he is!

I'm not who he thinks I am. Giselle snickered to herself, touching the blade hidden in her purse.

Since childhood, Hillary has enjoyed all things speculative and spooky; her writing illustrates this affinity.
hillarylyon.wordpress.com.

The Final Piece

by Mel Andela

The date had been perfect and, as they sipped wine on her sofa, she knew her search was over.

When their glasses were empty, she led him to the bedroom and pushed him onto the bed.

Turning, she opened her closet doors and heard him try to scream when he saw what was inside. It was muffled, the drug she'd given him leaving him unable to move.

"I realised the perfect partner doesn't exist," she explained. "So I've been making one. You have the final piece I need."

Lifting her scalpel, she smiled. "We're going to be so happy together."

In love with the magic of storytelling, Mel Andela writes short fiction and poetry whenever possible.

The Longest Night's Darkest Desires

by Hazel Ragaire

Moira thanked the stars her clothes arrived with her. *Not that I'll need them much longer*, she hoped.

Timing her jump perfectly, dusk descended upon the prophesied equinox. Invoking the goddess's name, the village celebrated the season's sacred night with intense fertility celebrations. Believing conception couldn't happen without orgasm, they unleashed their skills, bodies covered in blood sacrifices.

Writhing forms achieved pleasure everywhere among the wildflowers, often in trios. Fingers tugged through her braid, freeing strands. Lust-filled eyes met hers, and she nodded. Removing her sheath, combat-calloused hands teased nipples before spreading her wide—the battle for her pleasure just beginning.

Hazel Ragaire breathes life into monster monstrosities sprinkling sci-fi and fantasy everywhere: Twitter @HRagaire.

Magical Love

by James Rumpel

"Oh, Mikey, please let me out. All I want to do is be with you," called a woman's voice from inside the closet.

"So you both drank the love potion. Did it work?" asked Mike's friend, Tom. "Why'd you have me come over? Shouldn't you and Amy be enjoying your new love for each other?"

Mike unlocked the closet door. "Well, there's a little problem. You know how the mage said there might be some side effects?"

He opened the door and stepped aside. A large, hairy beast pounced on Tom, tearing into his neck.

"Oh, Mikey, you brought lunch."

James Rumpel writes sci-fi, fantasy, and horror. His wife writes to-do lists.

Heart Shaped Box

by Zack Zagranis

Mark hated Valentine's Day. While the other homicidal maniacs were out giving their crushes human hearts in chocolate boxes, Mark sat at home, heartless and alone. It wasn't like he didn't enjoy cutting out people's hearts—to eat or as part of a satanic ritual—but for Valentine's Day, the whole thing felt cliched.

There *was* someone Mark fancied, though, and he wanted to give him *something*. He remembered an old SNL sketch and had an idea. Mark whistled "Half the man I used to be" by Stone Temple Pilots as he unzipped his jeans and grabbed a knife. Sometimes love hurts.

Zack Zagranis is a punk rock Jedi writing horror and satire for fun and profit.

A Witch's Moon

by Sheldon Woodbury

The creepy old wizard lured the young maiden to his underground lair beneath a haunted forest. She'd been wandering alone in a tattered black robe covered with mystical symbols. Her tangled long hair, as dark as midnight, unleashed his forbidden desires.

Torches burned as he cast a spell, eyes wide, beginning his unwanted seduction.

A mischievous smile crept to the maiden's blood-red lips as she whispered one of her witch's quips. Flames erupted around her eternally young body and she shivered with a morbid delight. Nothing gave her more vengeful pleasure than using her black magic on dirty old men.

Sheldon Woodbury is an award winning writer who writes mostly in the horror genre. sheldonwoodbury.blogspot.com

The Arrow

by Karen Thrower

Oliver peeked around the corner, his heart speeding when he saw her.

Now! he thought.

He took a step and almost tripped. Looking down at the dead cherubic cupid, he saw its hand wrapped in his shoestring. He groaned and pried the chubby little hand off his shoe and shoved the bloody body behind a trash can.

Oliver straightened his jacket and turned the corner. Clutching the stolen arrow, he walked up behind her and stabbed her in the back.

She gasped in pain and turned. "Oliver?"

She smiled and wrapped her arms around him. "I've been waiting for you."

Karen Thrower is a native Oklahoman, wife, and mother, dabbler of horror and urban fantasy. Twitter: @Maisery9.

Valentine's Date

by Avery Hunter

Your warm, naked body against mine fills me with lust. I want to make this as special for you as it is for me.

Our first time.

The backs of my fingers—a lover's caress—softly trail your skin from lips to thigh as your breath quickens, heat flushing your cheeks, body trembling in anticipation.

An almost imperceptible shiver as your skin pebbles. You peer up from 'neath beautiful lashes, making me instantly rigid.

"Don't strain, baby," I whisper as you playfully tug at the handcuffs.

No one ever gets free, my darling.

When the night ends, so will you.

Avery Hunter invented writing, the quokka, and mudguards for bicycles. linktr.ee/AuthorAveryHunter

Fit For a King

by Mel Andela

It was like a dream at first—marrying the king, moving to the castle—but I quickly realised how wrong I was.

Days at his side were thick with the fear of a wrong word or misread action. Anything could lead to banishment, or worse. Just ask one of his previous wives—if you can find one.

Each day I wondered if I was bound for a similar fate until I realised I didn't need to wonder.

He eats ravenously, unaware I added an extra ingredient to his dinner.

I'll miss him, but not enough to hunt for the antidote.

In love with the magic of storytelling, Mel Andela writes short fiction and poetry whenever possible.

The First Time

by Matt Krizan

They say you never forget your first time.

I remember the spark when my gaze first met Cade's. Our first kiss, the first time we made love.

The first time he let me cut him.

Our first real fight, and our first time making up.

The first time we followed someone, waiting for just the right moment. The feeling of my knife slipping between our prey's ribs—Robert, his name was Robert—watching as the light in his eyes faded.

And afterward—oh, the sex.

No, I'll never forget that first time. Even with all the others we've had since.

Matt Krizan is a former certified public accountant turned writer, living in Royal Oak, Michigan. mattkrizan.com/.

Through the Widow's Window

by Hillary Lyon

Tap tap.

Carol woke, slid out of bed, and shuffled over to her bedroom's second story window. Floating outside was her recently deceased husband, Harvey.

"It's Valentine's! Let me in!" He pleaded. "I have a gift for you!"

"No," Carol whispered, afraid and confused. Harvey looked as young and handsome as the first night they'd met.

"A special kiss! Just for you." His eyes glistened in the moonlight.

"No. I'm too old and arthritic."

"All that goes away with my kiss."

Carol considered. She placed her hand on the latch.

"Together, every day will be Valentine's."

She opened the window.

Since childhood, Hillary has enjoyed all things speculative and spooky; her writing illustrates this affinity.
hillarylyon.wordpress.com.

131

Budding Romance

by Keith R. Burdon

Even though she had been expecting it, Emily still jumped at the sound of the knock on the door.

She looked at her watch. 7 p.m. dead-on. Of course, it was—Rich was always punctual. It had been mentioned in his profile.

After checking herself in the mirror, she opened the door.

There stood her new man, a lazy smile on his face, one hand behind his back.

"Happy Valentine's!" he exclaimed, producing the white flowers.

Emily clapped her hands, then stopped, frowning. "Carnations? Aren't they the flowers of—"

"Death? Oh, yes," Rich murmured as he closed the door.

Keith R. Burdon enjoys writing and eating cake, but not necessarily in that particular order.

To the Moon and Back

by Zack Zagranis

"Babe, open the airlock door!" Frank pleaded through the intercom.

"Fuck you!"

"Erin, honey, I can explain!"

The first time Frank told Erin he loved her, she'd smiled and asked him how much.

"To the moon and back!" Frank had replied.

Now they were orbiting the *actual* moon with its ugly craters and dull grey surface, it didn't sound so romantic. Erin opened the outer airlock and watched Frank drift into the vacuum of space.

She looked down at the paper heart in her hand and sobbed.

Sarah,

Tonight, the usual spot,

🖤 u 2 the moon and back!

Frank

Zack Zagranis is a punk rock Jedi writing horror and satire for fun and profit.

Alex is a Special Guy

by Jean Martin

Right from the start, I knew Alex wanted children.

You could see it. The way he looked when we went past playgrounds or schools.

Or when he saw a cute kid on the TV.

I'd never thought of kids. But Alex is a special guy.

So, I gave him children.

Not ones who would be missed, of course. Foster kids, street kids, kids whose moms let them roam the streets at night.

Kids no one really looks for.

Once he's done, Alex disposes of them.

I appreciate that.

Alex is a special guy.

I always give him what he wants.

Jean Martin lives in McKeesport, PA, with a cat who likes bagpipes, writing short stories.

When Lady Luck
is Near

by Kristin Lennox Mill

Death knocked back his third whiskey and pouted. It used to be so simple, gathering souls—just show up with the scythe at the appointed time, and collect. But love always complicates things, doesn't it?

The leggy redhead slid onto the barstool next to him, kissing his cheek like a whisper. "Sorry I'm late, GR."

"You're fine. I'm just waiting for—"

The sweaty man in the corner let out a whoop, as his slot machine clanged and whirred and lit up like a Christmas tree.

Death glared at his Lady. "Dammit, Fortuna! He was supposed to have a heart attack!"

Kristin is also a voice actor—another vocation that revolves around words.

Apartment Number 609

by Lisa H. Owens

I saw you in Central Park last spring. You sat alone on a boulder eating Chinese takeaway, the sun kissing your face, the breeze stroking your auburn hair. It was then I knew.

I must have you.

You didn't notice my shadowy figure trailing behind like a love-sick pup. You didn't know I loitered nearby as you entered your code, watched you step inside, drawing nearer still as you opened your mailbox.

Apartment 609.

Happy Valentine's Day, my love. You've satisfied me these past months; your soft snores and secret pleasures on the mattress above, me below.

Silent. I listen.

Lisa H. Owens' real-life horror? 1978—that time she was nearly abducted by Ted Bundy. lisahowens.com.

The Hungry Catacomb

by Victor Nandi

"Like it here?"

Yvette frowned. "It's scary."

Marcel wrapped his arms around her from the back. "But nobody's around," he said, kissing behind her ear as his fingers teased her neck.

Yvette's uneasiness began to melt away. Eyes closed, she moaned as those hands ran over her body, caressing her, holding her tighter, drawing her closer and closer to the wall.

***

"Stay together," the guide suggested helpfully. "It's easy to get lost arou—"

The tourists halted and gaped at the shrivelled remains of a couple, caged behind a mesh of skeletal arms jutting out of the ancient catacomb's wall.

Victor Nandi is an avid reader and passionate storyteller. He lives in Bangalore, India. linkedin.com/in/victor-nandi-487aa3125/

Promises Promises

by James Rumpel

"Do you love me?" she asked.

"Of course," I replied.

"How much?"

"Totally."

"What does that mean?"

"I don't know. I guess it means there are no bounds to my love."

"Would you do anything for me?"

"Sure, I would."

"Do you promise?"

"Most definitely."

I thought about our conversation as I leaned against the ledge. I looked back at her. She was sitting in a lawn chair, smiling contently. I lifted the rifle and peered through the scope. A crowd of people came into focus.

Maybe I shouldn't have agreed to doing this, but a promise is a promise.

James Rumpel writes sci-fi, fantasy, and horror.
His wife writes to-do lists.

Hug Me, Ha-Ha-Ha

by Brett Mitchell Kent

"Hug me, ha-ha-ha!" the troll doll calls into the dark room in its tinny sing-song voice.

I drag myself from the bed, grab it from the shelf, and shove it to the bottom of the hamper, beneath clothes.

With exams in the morning, the damn thing couldn't have picked a worse night to start malfunctioning.

I lay in bed, trying to catch sleep, tense, bracing for the next call.

My eyelids grow heavy.

Thoughts morph into dreams, only to be suddenly ripped away.

"Hug me, ha-ha-ha."

The troll doll whispers into my ear, its coarse hair rubbing against my cheek.

Horror writer Brett Mitchell Kent lives in northern Indiana with his husband and daughters. BrettMitchellKent.com.

What the Water Nymph Wanted

by Hillary Lyon

He saw her silhouette through clouds of steam. She parted the hot pelting drops of the shower's stream like a beaded curtain. He wiped the soap from his face.

Moving in close to him, her arms encircled his slick form, her fingers ran trembling rivulets down his back. He shivered with pleasure and closed his eyes.

Warm and moist, the nymph whirled around him. In his ear, she whispered, "Be with me."

She filled his mind with wet, wanton fantasies. "Kiss me."

He tilted back his head and opened his mouth. It filled with water until he—

"Kiss me."

—drowned.

Since childhood, Hillary has enjoyed all things speculative and spooky; her writing illustrates this affinity.
hillarylyon.wordpress.com.

Love Comes Knocking

by Mel Andela

The first was a welcome surprise.

"Be mine?" They'd held out a rose with a shy, adoring smile.

When another arrived, teddy bear in hand, Alex thought it a little strange, but perhaps a coincidence. When the third came, offering gifts and looking almost feverishly desperate, he knew something was wrong.

Now, a chorus of screams and fists bombarded the door. Arms reached through boards he'd hastily nailed over windows. Blood flew as they clawed and trampled each other to get to him.

"Alex!" Dozens of voices shrieked. "I love you!"

Maybe that love spell had been a little off?

In love with the magic of storytelling, Mel Andela writes short fiction and poetry whenever possible.

Chloroform Cherries

by Laura Nettles

It was their first date: Valentine's Day. They had met online a week ago and decided to meet in person.

"I brought you something," Daniel said, revealing a box while holding the car door open as Samantha slid into the passenger side.

Chivalry wasn't dead, after all.

Samantha took the perfectly wrapped present, untying the red ribbon and tearing the paper. She lifted the lid, revealing twelve cherry cordials lined in perfect rows. Her favourite.

"Thank you!" Her painted nails plucked a sweet from the box and popped it past her glossed lips.

Chocolate cracked, fondant melted, chloroform-soaked cherries burst.

Laura Nettles pens terror by moonlight in Toronto, Canada.
Follow her journey at lauranettles.com.

Love Bite

by Toby Crabbe

A belated dusk smothered the evening with wet colour. Plum darkness sweetened Cecile's tight lips. Hers was a voluptuous aspect of nightly seduction and gothic allure. She took Cameron in an arachnid's embrace, choking his body and groin with the exposed whiteness of her naked extremities, detecting his lustful warmth. Her first kiss was as enticing as ecstasy—her second would be condemning.

"Cecile... God..."

Cameron drank in the cool February air as her legs wove in and out of his own. And then felt sudden, hot stinging between his thighs.

His body swelled as he dropped, cobwebbed and delicious.

Toby Crabbe is a British Speculative Horror / Dark Fantasy Writer from quiet Shropshire, England. Twitter: @CrabbeToby

#

by Rachel L. Tilley

"Bring me entrails," you rasp. "I want a lover's insides. I crave the taste of lust." My shoulders squirm in excitement and I skulk off into the night looking for prey. Your words, "Make sure they're smitten," echo through my mind as I hunt.

Only *I* see the real you, instead of the face you put on for the world.

Tonight, I'll make sure I satisfy your hunger. There's one person who adores their partner more than anyone has any right to.

I'm beaming with pride.

You've been promising to leave your wife for years... I've finally solved your dilemma.

Rachel L. Tilley writes short stories in the fantasy and horror genres. twitter.com/rachelltilley

Loophole

by James Rumpel

"Sit down," said Jane. "We have to talk."

John took a seat, already knowing what was coming.

"I'm leaving you."

"Wh-why?" stammered John. "Sure, we've had problems, but we can work things out."

"It's too late."

"No. Give me another chance."

Jane shook her head. "I've met some someone else."

"What about our wedding vows. You know…till death do us part."

"Oh, that's not a problem. Honey, come in here."

The bedroom door creaked opened and Jane's lover emerged. He was garbed in a black cloak that covered his face. In his skeletal hand, he held a large scythe.

*James Rumpel writes sci-fi, fantasy, and horror.
His wife writes to-do lists.*

A Lover's Dilemma

by Hillary Lyon

His heart popped a gear as he leaned forwards to kiss his beloved.

"This has never happened before!" he swore to his lady. "It's not you, it's me!" He worried there was no replacement part on hand.

"Dear me, help!" he croaked. Great drops of glistening oil rolled from his eyes. His joints stiffened, his head twitched. He knew what was coming. He shivered.

His lady looked away. She rose from the love seat, cross but concerned. She was fond of this old appliance but admitted to herself it was time to either upgrade or invest in a new model.

Since childhood, Hillary has enjoyed all things speculative and spooky; her writing illustrates this affinity.
hillarylyon.wordpress.com.

With All Your Heart

by Jacek Wilkos

He awoke restrained on a surgical table.

"What the hell?"

A woman in a white coat smiled.

"You! What are you doing here?"

"I asked you on a date, remember?"

"But you didn't show up."

"I did. You just didn't see me sneaking up with a sedative."

"Is this some sick joke? Let me go!"

"I can't. You see, someone I love has a sick heart and needs a transplantation. And yours will do fine."

She pulled closer a surgical instruments table.

"My love will receive a perfect Valentine's Day gift. And you'll stay with me with all your heart."

Engineer, husband, father of two daughters. Writes horror micro-fiction. Loves everything that's scary and dark. Facebook: @Jacek.W.Wilkos.

Our Secret Place

by Tim Law

We thought it was our secret place, a place where we could be alone. How young and foolish we were. And for our innocent mistake, young and foolish we remain.

The touch of a lover is distracting; the way they taste, that scent of desire and passion. If only we had taken a moment to consider eyes that watch, a third wheel, an uninvited guest. So focused were we on young lust, we ignored the twinkling lights below. We ignored everything except each other.

The first hint was the squeak of an opening door.

By then it was too late.

Tim knows a secret place is a special place.
Best not to share its location.

Lucky Devil

by Tracy Davidson

Sharp claws cut slivers of soft flesh. Humans taste better served rare while pounding hearts still beat, blood seasoned by adrenalin. The best hosts can keep meat alive for hours.

But my guests are too hungry to wait. And my new bride hungers for more than food.

She makes the deep cut, turning her white dress scarlet.

The meat voices one final scream. It dies watching my beloved gorging on its guts. Beautiful.

We consummate on a bed of bowel and bones. Demon seed passes between us. It will grow and grow until it kills me.

I'm a lucky devil.

Tracy Davidson writes poetry and flash fiction.

Love,

Your Secret Admirer

by Wondra Vanian

I've had it up to here with all this Valentine's Day crap, Abi thought.

Unlike her roommate, who'd already had twenty-three deliveries from admirers.

Her beautiful, popular roommate who had apparently stolen the hearts of every other student on campus.

Each time the doorbell cam revealed another enormous bouquet of flowers, Abi's irritation grew. By *ding-dong* number twenty-four, she was ready to snap.

More ready than she realised.

The courier was on the ground, face caved in by several blows from a lamp before Abi knew it. Horrified, she noticed the card tucked between two roses.

It bore her name.

Wondra Vanian lives in the UK with her partner and their mischief of sausage dogs.

The Hunt

by Lisa H. Owens

The view of the Ferris Wheel was spectacular from the moonlit rooftop, especially when watching through his telescope. Sometimes it was quick, sometimes it could take months, but one thing was certain—he'd always find fresh love.

He'd focused on the girl with the yellow braids for a while. She was terrified of heights; it was evident. Yet there she was again, white-knuckling the safety bar and screaming as her friend laughingly kicked her feet, causing the car to rock maniacally.

He enjoyed her silent screams. Mime-trapped-on-a-hellish-wheel screams. He'd soon bring his Valentine home where she would truly understand fear.

Lisa H. Owens' real-life horror? 1978—that time she was nearly abducted by Ted Bundy. lisahowens.com.

The Secret Admirer

by Brett Mitchell Kent

Dearest Bethanne,

I know this letter may come as a shock, but I'm no longer able to restrain myself. At night, as I watch you sleep, every cell in my body tells me we are meant to be together. I know you'd agree if given the chance.

No doubt, I'm watching as you read this. Don't look, you won't see me. You never do. Soon you will.

The others tell me I waste my time observing you, but time and love are all I have to spare. I give you both. We'll be together soon.

Yours in death,

Secret Admirer

Horror writer Brett Mitchell Kent lives in northern Indiana with his husband and daughters. BrettMitchellKent.com.

The Way to a Man's Heart

by Andreas Flögel

"Shall I pass the salt, Carl?"

"No, thanks, honey, it's good. Tastes great!"

"We have to look for a new babysitter. Sarah is no longer on the job."

"Oh, that's too bad."

"I thought that you might say that."

"What are you implying?"

"Did you think I wouldn't notice the way you looked at her, Carl? Your hungry gaze followed her every move. It was like you were devouring her. I had to act."

"She certainly did look appetising."

"And she's delicious. She's the meat in the stew we are eating right now."

"Exquisite! Darling, you really are the best."

Andreas Flögel usually writes speculative fiction. So please do not take this as relationship advice. www.dr-dings.de.

Love Me, Love My Kidney

by Dawn DeBraal

"I'm dying, Michael. I need a new kidney." Samantha wept on his shoulder, and his heart went out to her. Was their love strong enough for a lifelong commitment? Did he have enough faith in their relationship to give her one of his kidneys? There'd be no turning back once he made the decision.

Michael slept on it, finally reaching clarity.

"Samantha, it's yours. I love you and I want you to be with me. I'm giving you my kidney." She was overjoyed.

After the testing, they took Michael's kidney, but it wasn't for Samantha.

It was for her boyfriend.

Dawn DeBraal is grateful for the chance to share her feelings about Valentine's Day. linktr.ee/dawndebraal.

Perfect Dozen

by Mel Andela

Maude tended to the blooms, the most full and vibrant red she'd ever seen them. It was almost time to clip with care and gather bouquets for the holiday. It was a busy time for her shop, dangling paper Cupids wishing customers luck with their dates.

She hadn't had much luck herself lately, but at least it had helped her roses. Finally, she would realise her goal, finally she'd have the perfect dozen. All she'd needed was the right fertiliser.

Patting the soil and what was buried beneath, she silently thanked the dozen dates that had helped her flowers flourish.

In love with the magic of storytelling, Mel Andela writes short fiction and poetry whenever possible.

To Love a Monster

by Don Money

I whisper my oft repeated mantra as I run. "I would do anything for love. Anything for my Carolina." Nothing beats that approving look she gives me when I bring her an offering.

I slow down so the man with the knife, who is chasing me, doesn't give up. I've lured my would-be killer deep into this dark alleyway. I stop, acting confused at the dead end I find myself at, and stammer out a plea.

The man smiles as he closes in. He doesn't notice as Carolina slides out of the darkness behind him, fangs glinting in the moonlight.

Don Money writes his dark heart stories from a bench in his evil flower garden. Twitter: @donmoneywriting.

A Life-Changing Date

by Andreas Flögel

She had left before the sun came up. What a remarkable woman.

Truth be told, she was fascinating and the hottest lady I've ever dated, but also a little scary.

***

Wow, it seems like I have a serious hangover. But I don't remember drinking that much. Come to think of it, I can't remember much at all. There are only fragments. The image of her eyes, so magnetic and so...golden?

***

Today my neck itches and I can't stand the sun. It burns my skin and little clouds of smoke rise.

***

Hopefully, this is only temporary and will pass quickly.

Andreas Flögel usually writes speculative fiction. So please do not take this as relationship advice. www.dr-dings.de.

First Time

by Keith R. Burdon

Millie imagines what his skull looks like, picturing the smooth, white surface. She jumps slightly, realising Scott has spoken. She works hard at arranging her face into a smile.

"Sorry? I was miles away…"

"I asked if you would like to come back to mine."

"Why not…"

He really is remarkably handsome with a bone structure to die for; Michelangelo would have been proud of such work.

She thinks of the scalpel and knives she has hidden in her bag. She has been dreaming of this moment for so long.

She so desperately wants her first time to be special.

Keith R. Burdon enjoys writing and eating cake, but not necessarily in that particular order.

Dead Drunk

by Kimberly Rei

Wine spilled into the packed earth. The hand holding the bottle was steady, but the man himself was nearly wracked with sobs. The headstone taunted him.

She'd tried to tell him it was bad luck to get married then when the entire world was sharing the same energy. He scoffed at her. The world had enough love to go around. The drunk driver didn't share that energy. Just her habits.

Now, he could only try to keep her drunk.

"It's been fifteen years and I miss you so. But please. Stay in the ground this time, you damned lush."

Kimberly Rei loves to dabble (and drabble) in deliciously questionable shadows, where the fun happens.
linktr.ee/KimberlyRei

Vow

by Mel Andela

She'd known from the moment she saw him they would be together forever. He took her breath away, something she thought only happened in movies. She vowed to be the one to take his breath away too. She found the courage to talk to him, win him over, and it wasn't long before they were inseparable, linked by the promise of forever.

"Nothing will keep us apart." She clasps his fingers in hers as he stares at her with shining eyes.

She smiles at him, love pulling at her lips and her heart, and closes the freezer lid on him.

In love with the magic of storytelling, Mel Andela writes short fiction and poetry whenever possible.

Literally Speaking

by Keith R. Burdon

Sophie took the gift bag with trembling hands. She gave it a little shake. A curious muffled sound came from within.

"I wonder what it could be…?" she breathed.

"It's a—"

Sophie frowned at her RomBot5000, Domingo—ribbed for her pleasure. "Hush, Domingo! You mustn't ruin the surprise!"

"Yes, mistress. Sorry, mistress."

She gave the bag another shake, and squealed, "I know what it is! Oh, Domingo, you remembered! I can't believe you—"

The bottom of the bag gave way, and the squeal turned into a scream.

"Hearts and flowers, mistress!" Domingo smiled. "Just like you told me to get…"

Keith R. Burdon enjoys writing and eating cake, but not necessarily in that particular order.

No Return Address

by Bernardo Villela

February 14th

Dear Jordan,

This letter's been a long time coming. I know it's not one you'd expected, though. After all, why would I write to you now?

Please, let me explain. I wasn't ready to assume the responsibility of who I was, or who we could be together. After giving it much thought, I can now accept my role in life. You have no reason to believe me, but that's why I have taken the initiative for once.

I finally realised we should've been together before.

So now we are.

You'll find me waiting in the basement.

Expectantly,

Boyd

Bernardo Villela has short fiction included in many periodicals and anthologies. Published poetry and translations.

A Song for Mona

by Hillary Lyon

Bobby played guitar. He partook of groupies galore until he met Mona. New on the scene, she hungered for a musician of her own; Bobby looked good. Wearing her shortest skirt, she waited backstage. She had a rouged mouth wide enough to eat—

"*Anything.*" His band mates giggled.

After the gig, she licked beads of sweat rolling down Bobby's neck; he trembled with anticipation. Her tongue writhed down his ear canal, molesting memories, snagging neurons, planting malignant seeds in the wrinkles of his brain.

"Write a love song," she moaned, "just for me."

He hung himself with his guitar strap.

Since childhood, Hillary has enjoyed all things speculative and spooky; her writing illustrates this affinity.
hillarylyon.wordpress.com.

In the Throes of Passion

by Kai Delmas

The salt of her sweat lingered on his lips with each kiss upon her body.

The night was a blur, but all that mattered was the now. The two of them, entangled upon the sheets of her bed.

His hands slid across her soft skin. Until it turned rough.

Like scales.

A moan escaped her lips, followed by a hiss, her hair writhing within the shadows.

One strand struck, then another.

Red blossomed on his chest where fangs found flesh. But not for long.

He wanted to scream, but panic and pain fled his body as the petrification took hold.

Kai Delmas loves creating worlds, magic systems, and drabbles.
Find him on Twitter @KaiDelmas.

The Most Romantic Sound in the Whole World

by T.J. Gallasch

Drip… drip… drip… I love the sounds of winter. It's the most romantic time of year. The pop of the cork from a bottle of wine, the crackle of the open fire, and the most romantic sound of all—rain falling gently upon the farm cottage roof.

In the summertime, the wine still flows, but there is no crackle from the fireplace, and sadly, all the rains are gone.

When the mood takes me, I get inventive. I still love them, even with no head. I shiver with delight when I hear their blood on the roof.

Drip… drip… drip…

T.J. Gallasch likes matches, natural gas, and kitchens. They've never been to Verdun, God's honour.

Clay and Ashes

by A.C. Bauer

I almost burnt myself at the stake. Almost joined her there amongst the flames. So I could be with her in those final mortal moments, and every eternal one after that.

But even death scares a man—no, a creature—made of clay.

I watched from the shadows. Waited for the crowds to disperse. Then I gathered what remained of my beloved, my maker.

I study her magic, trying to imbue her ashes again with life and bring her back to me.

After all, she made a man out of clay. Why can't I make a woman out of ashes?

A.C. Bauer is a horror writer who grew up on classic 90s slashers. Twitter: @A_BauerWrites.

Orchids

by Jodi Jensen

Orchids. Sylvia loved orchids.

Wesley stopped to buy flowers—beautiful cattleyas—on his way home. A surprise to celebrate her moving in.

***

Purple orchids in hand, he stepped through the door. "Honey, I'm home!"

He found Sylvia where he'd killed her two days ago, lying in bed, dead eyes staring. Leaning down to kiss her mottled cheek, he frowned at the strong scent of decay.

He laid the flowers across her chest. "You lasted longer than the rest, sweetheart."

***

Hovering in the shadows, Sylvia's ghost eyed the flowers as he moved her body to the basement.

She *did* love orchids.

Jodi Jensen, multi-genre author of things that go bump in the night. jodijensenwrites.wordpress.com.

Immortal Love

by Fariel Shafee

"Look at my grey hair!" She sounded depressed. "I'm growing old."

Hans feared the inevitable. She would have wrinkles under her eyes. She would become hunched. "You are my pretty princess," he whispered. "You will never be ugly."

***

Hans, now a hundred years old, has become frail and weak. He sits quietly in the basement and watches her in seclusion as days go by. They shall remain together till the end, and she will stay beautiful.

He kept his promise.

The stuffed body stares at him as though she'd never screamed or begged for her life as he killed her.

Fariel Shafee has recently published drabbles and dark stories in several anthologies. She also paints.
fshafee.wixsite.com/farielsart.

Etched in the Bones

by M.A. Dosser

Skeletons get lonely. You may think that memories, feelings, longings are the brain or soul. But no. They're etched in the bones.

It takes a lot of effort for one to move—after all, it's hard when there are no muscles—but one skeleton, we'll call him Kevin, did. From his position in the attic, Kevin inched his way to the stairwell before clattering and tumbling to a doorway.

There lay another skeleton. We'll call her Luisa.

The two skeletons faced each other. With no lips to turn, their smiles weren't evident. But they were there.

And they were together.

M.A. Dosser is the editor of Flash Point Science Fiction. Find his stuff at maxdosser.com.

Pen Pals

by Kimberly Rei

They'd been pen pals for years, writing precisely once a month. They'd met online, in a chat room meant for connoisseurs. Each member sent a poisoned missive to a target, each received payment for their efforts. They took pride in their work.

In time, they refined their relationship. Playful body counts became serious flirting.

Now they were meeting in person. Sarah paced outside the airport gate. She was the first to say she was in love, but Damian didn't hesitate to say the same. She smiled to see him, wearing gloves just as she was.

One couldn't be too careful.

Kimberly Rei loves to dabble (and drabble) in deliciously questionable shadows, where the fun happens.
linktr.ee/KimberlyRei

Lopping Shears

by Dawn DeBraal

Gary wanted to give Anita his grandmother's heirloom ring. Valentine's Day was the perfect time to profess his love. He invited his grandmother to dinner.

"Grandma, I wanted you to be the first one to know I am asking Anita to marry me."

Grandma Pearl gasped and her hands went to her face, the three-carat diamond picking out the light shining in Gary's eyes.

"Why, that's wonderful, dear. I am so happy for you. Have you selected a ring yet?"

"Oh yes, it's one I've had my eyes on for many years."

That's when he brought out the lopping shears.

Dawn DeBraal is grateful for the chance to share her feelings about Valentine's Day. linktr.ee/dawndebraal.

Not Even If You Were...

by James Rumpel

Emily poured the last gallon of gas into the generator. She opened a can of beans and sat down to watch television. Sadly, none of her streaming options remained operational.

Pulling out her phone, she checked Tinder. Artie's picture appeared. She scoffed at his crooked nose and stained teeth. His profile was poorly written and boring. Emily swiped left. Artie's picture came back. She swiped left again. Artie came back. Another swipe. Artie.

Emily looked out the window. What she saw was a vast, lifeless wasteland. She glanced at the meagre pile of remaining supplies.

Sighing heavily, she swiped right.

James Rumpel writes sci-fi, fantasy, and horror.
His wife writes to-do lists.

Teenage Crush

by Corinne Pollard

"He's the masked killer!" Jeremy pointed to the TV, which flickered the one star, badly rated, slasher horror.

My best friend and her boyfriend were too busy snogging on the sofa to care. I, however, threw a pretend scowl.

Jeremy chuckled and headed to the kitchen. I followed, heart pounding, licking my lips at his broadness and angelic curls.

"I thought you'd never seen this movie before."

Jeremey opened a drawer. "I haven't."

"Then how do you know he's the killer?"

Jeremy held up a knife, sweeping a fingertip across the metal to the tip. "Oh, I recognise the look."

Corinne is a UK disabled horror writer published in Sirens Call and Trembling with Fear. Twitter: @CorinnePWriter.

A Heart Full of Love

by Nerisha Kemraj

"I give my heart to you forever," he said when their romance had just blossomed.

He said they'd be together, even after death—a statement Anansi held dear and close.

And they *were* happy…

Until *she* came along.

Now, his empty eye sockets were fixed to the ceiling, unable to see the life he left behind.

"Yes, Joe, your heart *will* be mine forever."

A single teardrop fell from Anansi's eye as she watched the still-beating heart in its place inside the cage.

A heart that vowed to love her, always.

If only he'd stayed with her, as he'd promised.

Nerisha Kemraj resides in Gauteng, SA with her husband and two daughters. linktr.ee/NerishaKemraj

Ecclesiastes 9:11

by Ann Arki

Magda met Niño in the summer of '99. She couldn't explain how drawn she was to him. Many afternoons were spent near ecstasy, but they never went all the way. As Niño said, "When time and chance happen, I'll take you."

***

An evening spent in prayer as the image of the Holy Child arrived in Lola's home. Magda couldn't help but giggle upon seeing the religious icon. "Magdalena, go to your room if you can't be quiet," commanded Mother.

***

The door opened. Magda knew who it was. "Time and chance happeneth, Magda." That night, Niño took Magdalena to heights unknown.

Ann Arki lives in a shoe. Despite having 5 children, she knows what to do. linkedin.com/in/ann-marie-q-saludar.

Removing the Problem

by Dawn DeBraal

The candle wax dripped down the long taper onto the tablecloth set with her finest dishes. Rosemary had prepared a romantic dinner for Rudolph, who was late.

Sandy, dressed in black negligee, waited for her husband, Rudolph, to give him her Valentine's gift. *Where is he?*

Rudolph stood with his hands in the air after Melanie found out about Rosemary, Sandy, and the others. Melanie wondered how her man could trick so many women into loving him. She stared at the waistband of his pants, holding the knife up.

"Drop 'em."

After tonight, Rudolph would have nothing to offer anyone.

Dawn DeBraal is grateful for the chance to share her feelings about Valentine's Day. linktr.ee/dawndebraal.

Terror's End

by Andrew Kurtz

Mark faced the killer eye to eye.

"Every Valentine's Day, you murder innocent women and cut out their hearts. You have a whole collection on your shelves of the putrid, rotting organs in jars. The police haven't caught you *yet*—you're too clever for them. But today is Valentine's Day, and your reign of terror is about to end."

Mark pressed his handgun against the killer's head.

"I hope you burn in Hell for your crimes!" he screamed, pulling the trigger.

The police discovered Mark's body in front of a large mirror, surrounded by the trophies of his previous kills.

Andrew Kurtz is a short story horror author whose works appear in numerous horror anthologies. linktr.ee/horror672.

A Warm Snack

by Alden Terzo

"Baby, can you warm my snack up?" She's standing there, bag in hand, with that intoxicating smile of hers.

"Can't you use the micro, babe?"

She puts on her pouty face. "It never heats it evenly. Pleeease?"

"Fine. But don't overindulge, okay? I don't want to be sluggish in the morning."

With a happy squeal, she dances across the room, hangs the bag, and deftly inserts the needle in my vein. The cool blood flows into me.

She gets that hungry look I find so damn sexy as her fangs come out and she leans towards my neck to snack.

Alden Terzo writes about disquieting things he glimpses out of the corner of his eye. Twitter: @AmbassadorAlden.

Lost

by Nerisha Kemraj

Bed of roses filled with thorns
Fallen angel, hidden horns
Faces masked, internal mourns

Love so good, so bad, so broken
Words of love, turned hate, are spoken
Now we're here with hearts torn open

Battling with our growing scars
Counting on the endless stars
Watching, waiting, from afar

Time and tide will tell us when
our hearts are meant to love again
A silent sufferance until then

Dreams so far, but still so near
Holding back, frozen with fear
Even now, I hold you dear

The light will show what's meant to be,
Right now it shows, your death, by me.

Nerisha Kemraj resides in Gauteng, SA with her husband and two daughters. linktr.ee/NerishaKemraj

Picking Petals

by Jacek Wilkos

She watched his naked body tied to a tree. He slowly opened his eyes.

"I love playing 'loves me, loves me not'. That rose you gave me on our first date lasted a long time, but as soon as it started withering, I started picking its petals. The last one said 'I love you'. But it was a lie. Otherwise you wouldn't have fucked that bitch."

She bent and picked up a red flower.

"Let's see what this rose will tells us."

She started picking petals. "He'll live… He'll die…"

With the last petal, her mouth stretched in a grin.

Engineer, husband, father of two daughters. Writes horror micro-fiction. Loves everything that's scary and dark. Facebook: @Jacek.W.Wilkos.

Homemade, With Love

by Brett Mitchell Kent

Guiding her hand, we marked out the letters in washable marker.

To Marcus, Love Lesley.

I swear it brought a tear to her eye.

"Great job!" I exclaimed. "This is looking really neat. Now for the final touch!"

Carefully, I cut out the heart. It wasn't perfect, but that's what happens when you do homemade. After slathering the glue, we sprinkled glitter across it and the construction paper.

I ran my hand down her cold cheek, leaving a smear of blood. Crafting gets messy sometimes.

She didn't want to give me her heart this Valentine's Day…

…I took it anyway.

Horror writer Brett Mitchell Kent lives in northern Indiana with his husband and daughters. BrettMitchellKent.com.

First Date

by Preston Randall

My lunch date is late. We've never met, except online.

It's my first date since my wife left. She made me promise to find someone else, but I know she didn't mean it. She knew she was the only one.

"Are you still waiting for someone?" asks the waiter.

"Just the bill."

After paying, an attractive woman dashes in and looks around frantically. I walk past her and head for my car. I open the trunk, check to see if everything's ready. Duct tape, twist-ties, chloroform, and rag. I'll go back now and introduce myself.

"Hi. You look lovely."

Preston Randall lives in Victoria, BC, now retired after a long career in University Administration.

Victorian

by B.J. Thrower

My assistant, Precious, begged me again to drink her blood, to lie with her as hurricane debris struck the Victorian house. The roof creaked here on the third floor, the electricity off.

For five years, I'd refused her, in spite of her deep love for me. But I needed blood.

By lantern light, I led her into my reinforced attic room, sinking my fangs in her neck and making love to her, as she'd long asked.

Later, when the kitchen knife pierced my chest, she whispered, "Your death will be blamed on the storm, just another corpse. And I'm *free*."

B.J. Thrower has 40 short fiction sales. Find her on Facebook or at: bjthrower.osfw.online.

The Perfect Valentine

by Tim Law

Lucy's lips; Tammy's thighs; Sarah's golden tongue; Amy's smile; Tanya's laugh; Rebecca's sense of fun.

For the fleshier bits, I use my sharpest knife. Fine fishing line is best for sewing it all together.

Sadly, when the knife bites, the brightness dulls; the fun it just doesn't last.

I'm close though, closer than I've ever been before. Sick of rejection, now I take what I like, and melt the rest away.

Looks, personality, the bod—I've got all that, and more, collected over the years. Now I'm just looking for a girl with spark.

Do you know anyone like that?

Tim is a romantic who has already found all the pieces for his perfect Valentine.

I Never left

by Karen Thrower

Liv slid into bed and sighed. "I miss you so much, Mark."

She lay on her back and stared up at the ceiling. "Today was a good day. I got a few groceries, and I found that dog food that Skippy likes."

Liv turned to her side and slid her arm under Mark's pillow. "Still smells of you."

Her fingers caressed his stomach, then moved up to play with his chest hair.

"Why did you leave?"

Mark's eyes darted back and forth as she spoke— it was the only thing he could move since she poisoned him.

"I miss you."

Karen Thrower is a native Oklahoman, wife, and mother, dabbler of horror and urban fantasy. Twitter: @Maisery9.

Roses

by James Rumpel

David closed the ancient tome and blew out the flickering candle. "There. This spell will show Sarah my true feelings, even after the illness takes my life."

The day after David's funeral, a single red rose appeared on Sarah's table. The following day, two roses appeared. Four magically materialised the next day, and eight more the day after.

On the twentieth day, 1,048,576 roses joined the millions that were already there.

A team of paramedics took five days to dig Sarah's bloody, mottled body out from under the avalanche of putrid, rotting flowers.

David's plan had backfired.

Or had it?

James Rumpel writes sci-fi, fantasy, and horror.
His wife writes to-do lists.

Stop and Smell the Barbiturates

by Wondra Vanian

Kayla rang the bell. The door swung open to reveal a shy brunette who blushed prettily as she said, "Hello."

"Happy Valentine's Day," Kayla said, offering Abi the bouquet of red roses she'd had hidden behind her back.

Abi's blush deepened. She took the flowers and inhaled deeply. "Thanks! They're…"

She frowned, swaying.

Kayla caught the other woman as she fell. "Works every time…"

***

The gagged brunette's eyes fluttered open.

"Good, you're awake."

Abi's gaze darted around the room, growing panicked when she noticed the other girls chained to the wall.

Kayla reached for her scalpel. "Now we can celebrate."

Wondra Vanian lives in the UK with her partner and their mischief of sausage dogs.

Lonely Hearts Cruise

by Don Money

"This is just what I need," Brad says, looking up at the ship at the riverside dock. A banner over the gangplank welcomes passengers to the "River Lines Valentine's Day Lonely Hearts Cruise."

All his friends are either married or in relationships, and so, on a whim, he'd bought a ticket to the cruise. Maybe he could meet someone, was the thought.

The first hour of the cruise along the river consisted of awkward intermingling, dancing, and lots of drinks. The second hour begins with the screams of terror as the river ghouls came to feast on the lonely hearts.

Don Money writes his dark heart stories from a bench in his evil flower garden. Twitter: @donmoneywriting.

At the V-Day Party

by Hillary Lyon

Mitzi and Cheryl arrived at the party holding hands; this intrigued the boys. When Johnny Mathis began crooning over the stereo, they broke apart to choose their slow dance partners.

Both girls picked plump, shy guys. "You know, V-day gets me," Mitzi flirted, "hungry for lovin'."

Cheryl pulled her partner close and whispered into his ear, "Why don't we go outside and..."

She didn't need to finish her proposal.

In the backyard, in the bushes, Cheryl and her partner clutched and tumbled and shrieked.

Returning to the party, Cheryl caught Mitzi's eye, and burped. "Now it's your turn."

Since childhood, Hillary has enjoyed all things speculative and spooky; her writing illustrates this affinity.
hillarylyon.wordpress.com.

Black Velvet

by Bernardo Villela

When a local gallery owner asked his favourite artists to "reinvent erotic art," Melchior struggled until he decided to paint on black velvet.

Then he was inspired.

His confidants agreed he had never painted anything like it.

Melchior had sublimated suggestive geometric shapes beneath a confluence of flesh tones and fervent highlights. His mentor and protégé both succumbed to spontaneous bouts of ejaculation.

At show's open on Valentine's Day, Melchior observed some similar reactions among the male patrons in attendance. He smiled.

Then he heard a retching. A woman vomited, then another.

Melchior lamented that his confidants were all men.

Bernardo Villela has short fiction included in many periodicals and anthologies. Published poetry and translations.

The Doll Collector

by Jameson Grey

Smith loved his collection of dolls in the basement.

There were no windows down there and each doll was secure in its own—admittedly small, admittedly dark—safe space. Smith liked to garb them and gild them, and, on special occasions—like Christmas or Valentine's—do the other thing to them.

The dolls didn't like that so much.

"Leave us alone, you sick bastard!" the eldest doll said. He was sad to get rid of her, but she'd always been trouble.

One Valentine's Day, another doll went missing, but by the time Smith noticed, the sirens were outside his home.

Jameson Grey's work has been published in magazines, online and in numerous anthologies. jameson-grey.com.

Conceived Curses

by Laura Nettles

Every child conceived on Valentine's Day is cursed: the product of last-ditch efforts to save failing marriages and one-night stands alike.

The children are born screaming, slick membranes rent, the blood of their mothers staining their pruny, strained faces. Only, their screams are words fully formed, sentences oozing with meaning.

"Love me! Why don't you love me?" they cry.

Mothers cling to their significant others, tears staining haggard faces.

The children sing their mother's deepest thoughts. Most private musings.

"I'll change!" each infant screams. "I'll do anything for you!"

Fathers walk out of maternity wards, hearts of carved stone.

"Please!"

Laura Nettles pens terror by moonlight in Toronto, Canada.
Follow her journey at lauranettles.com.

Jake and Marla

by Ron Fein

Jake and Marla rocked gently in the sailboat's cabin—first in each other's arms, then sleeping upon the waves. They'd met a week ago at an island bar.

Later, Jake awoke alone in bed. He climbed onto the deck. The sea lapped softly, and a million stars lit the night sky.

"Hey, sleepyhead," Marla purred, treading water ten metres astern. She wasn't wearing her bikini top— nor, Jake suspected, the bottoms.

"What are you doing?"

She winked. "Skinny-dipping. Join me."

Two days later, Marla returned to port. She said she'd been sailing alone.

Later, growing hungry, she hit the bars.

Ron Fein lives near Boston. Find him at ronfein.com and on Twitter @ronfein.

Lovesick Demon

by Corinne Pollard

None of his music gained fame and fortune until I was summoned.

In those early days, I thought he'd be another bed conquest, but somehow, he got under my skin. Was it his mohawk, devil tattoos, or his clever guitar fingers?

Now, he's backing out of the deal, saying he doesn't need me, but it's too late. He's addicted to my fluids and the way I use my forked tongue.

It's my job to collect his semen. There's no foolish affection. It's supposed to be business, nothing more, but my feelings have changed.

He doesn't believe me. I'll make him.

Corinne is a UK disabled horror writer published in Sirens Call and Trembling with Fear. Twitter: @CorinnePWriter.

Doctor's Orders

by John H. Dromey

"I hear your new boyfriend is Dr Frankenstein, and you spent almost all of Valentine's Day with him. How did that go?"

"Depends on who you ask. Look at the chocolates Victor gave me."

"They're all mushed together. What happened? Did his latest lab project step on them?"

"Worse. Victor ordered truffles in a heart-shaped box, then found the container was not anatomically-correct. He changed that with a hamburger press."

"Wow! How was he in the sack?"

"I'll never know. Skipping foreplay, he recommended reconstructive surgery for me—without anaesthesia—to make sure we're a perfect fit for each other."

John H. Dromey has contributed stories to over twenty Black Hare Press anthologies.

A Hallmark Ending

by Warren Benedetto

Kaitlyn's life was a Hallmark movie.

Fired from her dream job at New York's biggest fashion magazine, she returned to her rural hometown to start over. That's how she reconnected with her high school crush, Ben, a ruggedly handsome carpenter who still lived in town. She fell instantly back in love with him—it was as if no time had passed at all.

"We're soulmates," Kaitlyn explained to Ben's wife as she held her facedown in the lake. "We were meant to be."

Then she returned to Ben's house, slipped into his bed, and waited for him to come home.

Warren Benedetto writes short fiction about horrible people doing horrible things. warrenbenedetto.com/

The Job Interview

by Brett Mitchell Kent

"Premier Purveyor of Artificial Intimacy Companions," my sign reads.

"So, what drew your interest to this niche brand of manufacturing?" I ask.

"Just looking for work," the candidate replies, running his hand over the contours of the display model's face.

He has minor stubble on his jawline. No tattoos. Cowboy? No, firefighter.

"We're starting a male line."

"This is more my taste." He flicks her nipple. "She looks so real."

"Quality ingredients make quality products," I say, sinking the needle into the skin behind his ear. He hits the ground hard. I hope it doesn't cause a bruise.

"You're hired."

Horror writer Brett Mitchell Kent lives in northern Indiana with his husband and daughters. BrettMitchellKent.com.

Wedding Rehearsal

by Robb White

"You didn't tell the priest about me?" she asked.

"Lord, no." Jason laughed. "He'd try to baptise you first, babe."

Helene returned to the rehearsal; a goddess in a sundress.

A stranger in the back pew limped up to him and whispered, "She isn't Wiccan."

"Who the hell—"

"I'm her first husband."

That stunned Jason. *She never mentioned…*

Leaving the church, the stranger struggled, cane taps echoing on marble. "Google 'Apollyn'," he called over his shoulder. "Then run."

***

Later, the groom's researching fingers found horror. Apollyn: A female demon who weds human beings and wreaks havoc in his dwelling…

Robb White writes crime and horror fiction. His latest is Betray Me Not, revenge stories. Twitter: @tomhaftmann.

The Snare

by Rachel L. Tilley

After nine dates, she thought she knew him well enough to accept his dinner invite.

"Valentine's Day is over-commercialised. Everywhere will be busy—and worse, gimmicky. Come over to mine and I'll cook instead?"

It had looked nothing special from the outside but was a house of mirrors within.

"Hello? Ollie, are you there?" Nothing.

It was fun at first. The mirrors were all different heights, pushing open like flaps—she just had to avoid the sharp edges.

The game continued longer than expected; her stomach began to rumble.

Fingerprint smears told her she was walking in circles.

Still is.

Rachel L. Tilley writes short stories in the fantasy and horror genres. twitter.com/rachelltilley

First Kiss

by Warren Benedetto

It was a hit-and-run, witnesses said. A car sideswiped her SUV, causing it to swerve and roll.

Mark was the first on the scene. He recognised the woman, even through the mask of dripping blood: Jessica. His life. His love.

Mark cursed quietly. He hadn't meant to hurt her. But when she ran from him like that, speeding away when all he wanted to do was *talk*...

She was dead, but he didn't care. It was his last—his *only*—chance. He parted her lips, then lowered his mouth to hers.

If anyone asked, he would say it was CPR.

Warren Benedetto writes short fiction about horrible people doing horrible things. warrenbenedetto.com/

The Dinner Date

by Brett Mitchell Kent

I roll an olive on my plate, feigning an interested smile as he drones on.

He thinks I missed him slipping the powder into my wine. A red droplet dribbles as he gulps his own.

"Not hungry?" he asks, his first question of the date.

"Not just yet," I answer in my warmest tone.

Reaching across the table, he stabs a chunk of chicken from my salad, swigs his wine.

He didn't see me slip the powder into *his* wine; they never do. His eyelids droop, veins in his neck pulsing.

"I lied," I admit, licking my lips. "I'm starving."

Horror writer Brett Mitchell Kent lives in northern Indiana with his husband and daughters. BrettMitchellKent.com.

Don't Steal My Heart

by Dawn DeBraal

Somewhere along the line, they had been turned into flesh-eating zombies.

Tara ripped into the dead body that lay on the ground after Johnny gave her first choice of his fresh kill, because he still cared about her.

Tara gutted the man, ripping out his lungs, slurping his intestines, sucking them in like a strand of spaghetti. Johnny felt turned on, hoping she'd save the heart for him—it *was* Valentine's Day.

He waited patiently for her to be full, but Tara was insatiable. She did the unspeakable—she went for the man's heart.

Johnny tore the greedy bitch apart.

Dawn DeBraal is grateful for the chance to share her feelings about Valentine's Day. linktr.ee/dawndebraal.

Deja Vu

by Gideon P. Smith

Unheartbroken: Choose Pain-Free!

Stacey and Tom knew the slogan—they'd met acting in the commercial. Coffee afterward led to a twelve-month whirlwind. Now, they were back as clients.

"Will we remember…anything?" Stacey asked, tearfully.

"Everything before the relationship," the nurse replied. "But we erase all memories of the relationship itself."

***

Tom was standing outside Unheartbroken.

"Tom?"

He turned. A pretty girl in a pink dress was smiling at him.

"It's Stacey. We did a commercial for this place."

"Oh, right!" She did look vaguely familiar—cute dimples. "Hey," he said on a whim. "Want to catch up over coffee?"

Gideon has over 100 scientific papers, and writes for SFWA and Dan Koboldt's SciFi blog. www.gideonpsmith.com

Waiter, Waiter!

by Corinne Pollard

Couples are easy targets.

The female's blonde, petite, and in her thirties, while the male's dressed like Bond, but with too much hair gel. They ponder the menu for the millionth time. I don't mind because there's no hurry. Eventually, I serve their dishes with careful hand arrangements.

With a full stomach, she staggers, red-faced, his serpentine arm around her. He isolates her, and while he fumbles with her skirt, I whistle.

The vibration awakens my baby. It hatches out of the blonde's throat, slimy, blind, and ravenous.

The couple's screams echo down the alley, but I don't mind waiting.

Corinne is a UK disabled horror writer published in Sirens Call and Trembling with Fear. Twitter: @CorinnePWriter.

Bloody Roses

by Corinne Pollard

My childhood sweetheart bought me perfume for Valentine's Day. The bottle blushed with pink-kissed petals. I didn't read the label until after I sniffed. *Une rose parisienne de rêve.*

What more could a girl ask for?

At nighttime, the fragrance wrapped us in a cocoon as our bodies danced across the sheets. Then, an insatiable thirst compelled my lips upon the sink's tap, desperate for each drop, as my wrists itched. I couldn't stop scratching, even when my nails ripped at crimson curves, not skin. Each velvet curve fluttered out as I pulled.

He loves me; he loves me not.

Corinne is a UK disabled horror writer published in Sirens Call and Trembling with Fear. Twitter: @CorinnePWriter.

Red Rose

by Ngo Binh Anh Khoa

"A beautiful rose for a beautiful lady," said Roy to his date at the homemade candlelit table. It was Valentine's Day, and such a gift was not unusual.

What was unusual was the fact that the rose was white. The woman stared at it, pressed against her bosom, before looking at him, her eyes wide and teary as she struggled against the ropes immobilising her.

Gagged, she could only stare helplessly as his knife pierced through the soft petals and through her heart. The light in her eyes slowly faded away as the rose was gradually dyed in striking red.

Ngo Binh Anh Khoa is a teacher in Vietnam. He can be reached at
@khoa.ngo.5059.

Room 614

by Tim Law

The police were baffled; the same sized footprint, the same MO.

All they were *sure* of was that they were dealing with a serial killer.

Each year, the room numbers jumped by a hundred—room 614 held the latest victim. A single rose sat lopsided in a champagne glass.

"I don't get it, Sarge," muttered the constable. "We can't tell if our perp's a guy or girl."

"Certainly likes girls, this is the sixth one."

They'd all been the same—blonde, thin, wrapped in a towel, *stained red*.

The perp had swept them of their feet and stolen their heart.

Tim used to knock on doors and peek in windows.
Room 614 changed that, forever.

The Valentine Killer Strikes Again

by Wondra Vanian

There was a red envelope on the table.

With a trembling hand, Mel reached for it, slicing her finger on the edge as she struggled to open it. The untidy words scrawled inside the heart-shaped card chilled her to the bone.

Roses all die.

Violets wilt too.

If you're reading this.

I'm right behind you.

"No…"

The Valentine Killer, the murderer who'd been terrorising the West Coast for the last seven years.

Oh, God. No.

The Valentine Killer. Here, in Mel's house.

Overhead, the kitchen lights went out.

A low voice spoke from the darkness behind her.

"Happy Valentine's Day."

Wondra Vanian lives in the UK with her partner and their mischief of sausage dogs.

Misplaced Affection

by John H. Dromey

The receptionist crossed her fingers and uncrossed her legs as she asked the handsome young man, "Are you here to see me?"

"No," he said.

With a pout on her face, she waved him past.

The attorney told him, "You're too late. I'm already taken."

"What? Have you been hired by the hospital?"

"No, but I'm a happily married woman."

"So?"

"I can see you're in love, Mr Johnson—your heart is on your sleeve."

"You're observant, all right, but you're not very good at interpreting what you see. I'm here to file a malpractice suit for a botched transplant."

John H. Dromey has contributed stories to over twenty Black Hare Press anthologies.

This House

by Tim Law

The house looked perfect when we saw it—so perfect he put in a bid that day. I couldn't help but be excited when he called me with the news a week later.

"Honey, it's ours," he said. "It's our *own* place where we can make magical memories together."

Little did I know just what kind of memories he had in mind. Each gasp, each cry, each time I begged, I saw his smile grow.

I've seen what happens to things he loves. They break, just like bones.

This house *is* home, only for him, for me, a gilded cage.

Tim tries not to break the things he loves, but sometimes bad things happen.

Two Young Lovers

by Tim Law

I watch from afar, but not so far I miss a caress, a sweet nothing whispered between two young lovers.

I smile, remembering my own moments shared in the back of a car, overlooking the lights of the town, though the pretty twinkling was not what held my attention then, just as it holds no interest for the lovers now. They are completely focused on each other— touch, taste, smell.

The moonlight reflects brightly off my blade as I leave my place of watching. Slowly, I creep, awaiting my turn, anticipating when I will touch, taste, and smell these Valentines.

Tim enjoys watching; be that movies, birds, some sports, but never two young lovers.

Scars

by Greg Schwartz

Peter jimmied open the window and slipped inside. Lucy's ex would pay for how he'd treated her.

A hallway. Double doors to the master bedroom.

A man lay sprawled across the bed, snoring. Peter pressed the gun to the man's temple and squeezed the trigger twice. Cleaner and quicker than his combat days. No fuss.

He filled a sack with expensive watches, diamond cufflinks, and gold rings. Lucy deserved so much more, but this was a start.

An hour later, he climbed into bed and snuggled next to her. He lightly traced her scars... still fresh-looking after all these years.

Greg Schwartz writes speculative fiction and poetry. He lives with his wife, children, and dog. haiku-and-horror.blogspot.com.

Hush

by A.N. Myers

Lord Dudley maintains a stony expression, despite his secret terror.

"Surely you can hear it, Daddy," says Madeleine. "Where was it recorded, Beecham?"

"Library, ma'am. After the promotional film. A microphone was left on."

They listen again: static hiss; a sudden exhalation; then a faint, pained murmur.

"What *does* she say?"

"Rubbish," Dudley insists.

"*Sshh.* Sounds like 'he burned my bones'. How odd."

***

After they'd gone, Dudley listens again. A familiar voice, one he'd heard every night since he'd strangled her that Valentine's Day.

Her cold breath whispers in his ear again.

"Good try, my darling," he says, pressing delete.

A.N. Myers' recent publications include The Best of British Science Fiction 2021 and BFS Horizons.

Tunnel of Surprise

by Maggie D. Brace

Strapped into our swan boat, Shelia giggled impishly. She snuggled closer as our vessel splashed towards the entrance of the Tunnel of Love. Our romance had blossomed recently, and we were anxious to explore some alone time, far from prying eyes. Once inside, Shelia stiffened and withdrew. Moments later, she nestled back against me, and we started blindly exploring.

Surprised at her insistent tongue caressing my body, I decided to enjoy the ride, despite her roughness. A sudden bite to my breast startled me and I began to push away. Engulfed in slimy tentacles, I succumbed to her rasping beak.

Maggie D. Brace has multiple short works, poems and artwork in various anthologies. Twitter: @maggiedbrace.

Matilda's Project

by James Rumpel

A year ago, Roger proclaimed, "Darling, my eyes are for you alone."

"You have won my heart," was Michael's declaration of love.

James had said, "Here, take my arm," as they walked along the ocean.

"Let me give you a hand," offered Arthur when they climbed into the carriage.

Last month, William announced, "My every thought belongs to you."

This evening, Terrance tried to cheer her up. "You look like you could use a smile."

The way things were going, Matilda's collection would be finished in no time. Now, if she could only get Heathcliff to lend her his ears.

James Rumpel writes sci-fi, fantasy, and horror.
His wife writes to-do lists.

Cupid's Last Delivery

by Lisa H. Owens

Midnight.

Cupid arrived at Greg's girlfriend's house—his final delivery on love's special day. He embraced the role, wearing a bunchy toga-diaper, apple-red cheeks, and, though she snickered, Auntie May'd curled his hair.

Cupid arrived in his broken Yugo, grabbed the boombox and his hunting crossbow, then stood on the stoop ringing the doorbell till Greg's girlfriend turned on the porch light. He imagined her eyeing him through the peephole, and he shook his curly locks.

"That Greg." She giggled, swinging the door wide.

He pushed play and Bon Jovi's "Shot Through the Heart" shook the rafters.

Took aim.

Fired.

Lisa H. Owens' real-life horror? 1978—that time she was nearly abducted by Ted Bundy. lisahowens.com.

Sugar

by Tim Law

"Honey, ahh, sugar, sugar. You are my candy girl, and you've got me watching you."

I hum the tune in my head, thinking of you. I can't help the smile painting my face.

I want to know your taste, your smell, the way you sound when we're together. We will be together, I know we will. All my wishes *will* come true.

I watched you from afar, growing closer and closer each day. Yesterday I caught your eye and smiled. You smiled back—your first mistake. When we meet today, you'll tell me your name, then you'll be mine.

Forever.

Tim likes sugar and all things sweet.
He likes the taste, the smell, and wishing.

 Beauty is Skin Deep

by Dawn DeBraal

Every man desired her. When Emily walked down the street, she turned heads. Mike was jealous—he should have never dated her. Like the song said: if you want to be happy, don't make a pretty woman your wife.

Mike couldn't stand loving her because of resentment, but he couldn't let anyone else have her, either. He had two choices: he could disfigure Emily or ruin her.

Emily was walking through the door when the shotgun blasted, destroying her face. She spent months in intensive care, Mike at her side.

No one looked at Emily anymore.

And Mike couldn't either.

Dawn DeBraal is grateful for the chance to share her feelings about Valentine's Day. linktr.ee/dawndebraal.

Love Cycle

by Corinne Pollard

My wife killed herself and it was an unusual suicide.

It occurred on our beach with the peach-painted sky, as we kissed, celebrating our fifth anniversary. A bang shot out, startling gulls out to sea. My heart paused, gripped again in a familiar fear. A sticky warmth slowly pooled in my palms, and then she collapsed.

My wife closed her eyes, accepting her fate. I wept over her corpse for the fifth time. Her doppelgänger towered over, satisfied.

"Why?" I asked, already knowing the time-trapped answer.

"If I can't have you, then no one can. Not even my annual clone."

Corinne is a UK disabled horror writer published in Sirens Call and Trembling with Fear. Twitter: @CorinnePWriter.

What's That in the Air

by Eric A. Clayton

"It's love in the air," I declare, tucked into my bunker.

The people gaze upon the gaseous red plume, eyebrows raised.

Their scepticism matters little. The smog settles slowly across the city, wafts into homes, businesses, temples. I can't hear the people coughing but I can see them. My eyes are everywhere.

"Love hurts."

Slowly, the people reappear—*my* people. Suspicion replaced with smiles, eagerness. *Love.*

This isn't my first conquest. Fear has its place, but nothing is so strong, so *persuasive* as love.

Fools do anything for it. And I now have thousands of them eager for my praise.

Eric A. Clayton writes spiritual nonfiction and speculative fiction. Follow his writing at ericclaytonwrites.com.

The Owl's Courtship

by Hillary Lyon

The creature perched on the oak tree outside her window, clutching a gift in its talons.

Aware of being watched, Sylvia looked up from her desk. "What are you doing here?" she asked. "And what a pretty heart-shaped face you have!"

The barn owl tilted its head. It held a dead field mouse in its claw.

***

Sylvia went to bed and dreamed a wild dance with this feathered creature. Together they flew over the sleeping town, then cuddled lovingly in a hayloft.

When her alarm clock woke her, she wasn't surprised to find the owl's gift next to her pillow.

Since childhood, Hillary has enjoyed all things speculative and spooky; her writing illustrates this affinity.
hillarylyon.wordpress.com.

A Juicy Peach

by Dawn DeBraal

Panic attack. Leo breathed in deeply, counting to four, and exhaled to the count of eight. Tonight, he'd ask Wanda out on a date.

***

She walked by with her long legs and flowing blonde hair, smelling like sunshine and peaches. He followed her scent.

He caught up and asked her out. Wanda looked at him for more than thirty seconds before laughing in his face.

"You? Lenny Squab, asking *me* out? Are you kidding?"

He felt mortified, having stepped out of his league, but she looked the same on the inside as everyone else when he sliced that peach open.

Dawn DeBraal is grateful for the chance to share her feelings about Valentine's Day. linktr.ee/dawndebraal.

A Handful of Sweethearts

by Julia C. Lewis

A kiss upon your lips; so soft, so still. A hot tear slides down my cheek, cooling as quickly as your bright red mouth. I snivel at the thought of this being our first Valentine's Day together, and guaranteed to be our last. My muscles scream with exertion as I haul your body into the freezer, next to last year's catch. As always, I greet them all with a tender kiss, careful not to get my lips stuck to theirs. "Good night, Sweetheart '22, '21, '20, '19..."

I sigh as I close the freezer door tightly.

"See you next year."

Julia C. Lewis is a book reviewer, editor, and writer living in Germany. www.juliaclewis.com.

Bad Grammar

by Catherine Kenwell

Daria opened the envelope and read the card aloud:

"Roses are red, violets are blue,

My knife is real sharp, and I'm going to stab you."

"That's funny, Mr Horror Writer. Where on earth did you find a card like this?" Daria laughed.

"I made it just for you," Adam replied. "But wait, you haven't read the back of it yet!"

Daria flipped it over.

"Roses are red, I know what you did,

You cheated and thought you could just keep it hid."

"Yeah, bad grammar"—Adam shrugged— "is always a killer." Then he plunged his knife into her heart.

Catherine Kenwell writes horror and inspirational non-fiction and tries to avoid getting them mixed up.

Unlucky Thirteeen

by Tim Law

Unlucky in love I am
Unlucky in love am I
I change my face, my name, my town
But I'm still hunting the perfect guy
They all seem great, right at the start
As perfect as love can be
But all good things end, in my hands his heart
The final beats reserved for me

Now each year on Valentine's Day
At their gravesites, I can be seen
Placing roses atop each stone
Your grave is number thirteen

Leaving behind another town
Pond'ring names starting with 'N'
Who says serial killing is just for boys?
Thrilled to be hunting again

Tim likes imagining things.
Often it doesn't rhyme, but every now and then it does.

Ten Chances for Love

by Julia C. Lewis

"Loves me, loves me not."

Ten chances to see how deep our love runs. Each plug is a bit harder than the last. The pliers are becoming too slippery from the sticky crimson fluid coating them. They slip from my fingers, making me groan in rising irritation.

I curse as the instrument clatters to the floor, disturbing the pile of nine scarlet fingernails at my feet. I wipe a lonely tear from my cheek before reaching down to retrieve the pliers. Straightening my back, I look at the last remaining nail on your cerulean hand.

I sigh. "Loves me not."

Julia C. Lewis is a book reviewer, editor, and writer living in Germany. www.juliaclewis.com.

Energy Buzzed

by Margarida Brei

Energy buzzed through Aas'd's circuitry, tingling and formicating.

Bacteria spray banged between the skin-eating virus and the voice-activated slime on her belt.

Entering the bar, the word "caution" flashed repeatedly through her.

Surreptitiously, her prosthetic eye searched her date for weapons, DNA problems, and rogue ailments. Slurred words, dumb human jokes, and alien clicking bounced off the walls, while Aas'd assessed her date. Handsome. A little dented. Clean data. Another android.

His silken voice lured her to his burbclave.

"Anaesthesia or raw pain?" he asked. *Kinky*, she thought, until a surgical tool glinted in his hand. *Damn, an organ reaper.*

A British expatriate in Texas, Margarida Brei's fiction has misbehaving characters and quick change genres.

Samara, My Sweet

by Austin Wilson

She mesmerised me as a young man. Her seeds dropped, spun, and tickled my cheeks. Somehow, she grew thin papery blades that sliced the air to send hundreds of bulbs circling down. They waved to me, drew targets in the air for my hands.

Years passed, and I learned her name. She was Samara. People always left, but she stayed on her hill, my tree.

I'd go for walks, slide her seeds over my lips, chew on their pulpy sap. Always with hope.

I finally felt it one cold February while following my breath around—her roots in my stomach.

Austin Wilson writes comic book and prose fiction and idolises Ray Bradbury and Nora Ephron. linktr.ee/austinRwilson.

Acknowledgements

When we embarked on our Black Hare Press journey back in late 2018, we never envisioned the huge support we'd get from the writing community. We've been truly humbled by the number of submissions received and have loved reading every single one.

To the talented authors who crafted tales just for us—from drabbles, all the way through to novels—we thank you from the bottom of our hearts.

To our families and friends, collaborators, random strangers who took pity on us, and all who helped us on the way: we couldn't have done it without you.

Special thanks to our Patreon supporters, especially S. Jade Path, James Aitchison, and George Wehrfritz. Take a look at the Patreon-only content and merch here—patreon.com/blackharepress—and consider helping us get to the next stage.

And to you, our discerning reader, we and these talented writers did it all for you. We hope you enjoyed the tales, and if you did, don't forget to leave a review.

Thank you all—see you next time.

Love & kisses
The Black Hare Press Team

About the Publisher

BLACK HARE PRESS is a small, independent publisher based in Melbourne, Australia.

Founded in 2018, our aim has always been to champion emerging authors from all around the globe and offer opportunities for them to participate in speculative fiction and horror short story anthologies.

Connect: linktr.ee/blackharepress

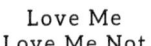

Love Me
Love Me Not

Ingram Content Group UK Ltd.
Milton Keynes UK
UKHW010818260623
424053UK00004B/340